CW01558536

BITTERSWEET LOVE

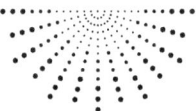

Q.B. TYLER

COPYRIGHT

© **2020 by Q.B. Tyler**

All rights reserved.
No part of this publication may be reproduced, distributed, or transmitted in any form or by any means, including photocopying, recording, or other electronic or mechanical methods, without the prior written permission of the publisher, except in the case of brief quotations embodied in critical reviews and certain other noncommercial uses permitted by copyright law.
This is a work of fiction. Names, characters, businesses, places, events, and incidents are either the products of the author's imagination and used in a fictitious manner. Any resemblance to actual persons, living or dead, or actual events is purely coincidental.

Cover Design: Cover Me Darling, LLC
Editing: Kristen Portillo—Your Editing Lounge

Vincent Maddox is the bane of my existence.

The cocky jerk with the God complex has made it his mission to make my life miserable since the day I moved to Chicago.

New job. New town. New start.

That is until my long-distance boyfriend decided to break up with me...via text.

Heart break can make you do stupid things. In my case, it made me drink way too much whiskey and hook up with my a-hole arch nemesis.

Vince Maddox is the bane of my existence...*or is he?*

*Bittersweet Love can be read as a standalone as a part of the Bittersweet universe

PROLOGUE

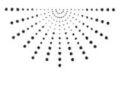

LAUREN

I'm sorry, Lauren. Please don't hate me.

I read the two sentence text message for the hundredth time today. My eyes well up as I feel my heart splitting apart inside my chest. I shut my eyes so I don't have to keep reading the soul crushing words, but still, I can hear them in my ear. I can feel them in my heart.

The distance is just too much.

I'm sorry.

I met someone else.

I'll always care about you.

I've been dating Drew Montgomery for the past year, despite leaving Atlanta and moving to Chicago. The plan was for me to get acclimated here and for Drew to join me once I was settled. We'd made plans for a future. One that included a ring that I had been staring at for the past four months on my Pinterest board. One that included a house I'd already found on quite possibly the cutest street in Chicago with an iron gate and gray shutters and a red door reminiscent of one I'd seen in *House & Garden* magazine.

It certainly did not include him falling for another woman.

I was planning our future, while unbeknownst to me, Drew had already written us as his past.

I tuck a dark brown hair behind my ear, my nervous tick I do when I'm uncomfortable and shift in my seat as my leg begins to bounce.

I'm sorry. I'm sorry. I'm sorry.

This is precisely why I did not want to get involved with Drew Montgomery. I knew he'd break my heart, but tale as old as time, I ignored my intuition and let myself get swept away by his sweet words and mind-numbing orgasms and promises for the future that he never intended to keep.

God, I am such a fucking cliché.

The familiar ping of my email sends my gaze away from my phone and towards my laptop only to see that it's an email from my boss with his edits attached to my latest piece. I don't have to open it to know that he'd bled all over it, but I'm feeling masochistic and this seems better for my mental health than stalking Drew's new girlfriend on social media, so why the fuck not?

I can barely see the red through my tears, the words blurring together so that it's just a mass of crimson on my screen.

"Holy shit, is Lauren Michaels, *crying*? And here I thought you had thicker skin than that."

A shiver snakes down my spine at the familiar voice. A deep voice that always tows the line between playfulness and condescension. I let out a breath, not prepared to deal with this person of all people.

Vincent Maddox is my arch nemesis.

The bane of my existence.

A know it all with an axe to grind because I flew in from Atlanta and created some competition amongst the "Boys Club" that is this sector of the NBC Network.

When I first got here, he'd just assumed I was an intern and spent the entire first week calling me *Laura* and barking his coffee order at me anytime we crossed paths. The look on his face when he realized we had the same job—*probably not the same pay, but that's another story*—was fucking priceless, especially since I was promoted from another location to essentially help with *his* job. He's spent every day since trying to undermine me or make me look incompetent in front of our bosses. Unlucky for him, he's never succeeded, and I enjoy making that known every time he fails.

He moves inside my cubicle, his overbearing yet sinfully smelling cologne wafting around me. It smells like bergamot and cedarwood and...*what is that?* I inhale deeply and try to ignore the spark igniting between my legs that comes from smelling a man who knows what kind of cologne will make a woman weak. He must peer over my shoulder because he speaks again and he leans on my desk revealing tanned muscular arms. "And over edits, no less?"

I glare at him, wondering how I appear to be in the mood for our usual battle of wits. "If you do not get the fuck out of my face in the next two and a half seconds, we will be spending the rest of the day in HR," I growl.

His lips curl into a playful smirk, and I'm instantly annoyed that my eyes move to his mouth and more importantly his perfect cupid's bow hidden beneath a layer of hair.

Vincent has one of those beards that is groomed but thick and full. Coupled with his muscular arms and broad chest, and the five inches he has on pretty much every man in the office, he looks like this sexual lumberjack masquerading as a writer.

"For me being in your cubicle?" He snorts and cocks an eyebrow before running a hand through his dirty blonde hair. "You don't have a leg to stand on."

"No, because I'm going to take that vase of flowers right there and bash your head in," I snap. I'd gotten dumped no less than five minutes ago; I'm crossing out of shock and into anger and Vincent Maddox is just the man that could send me into a blind rage. His piercing blue eyes narrow into slits as he leans off my desk. "If you're crying over edits, you're not fit for this job."

"It's not over edits, you pretentious fuck. And don't act like I'm not better than you at *our* job even on my worst day." I stand and even in my four-inch heels, I only come to his chest, so I crane my neck to glare at him. "Move the fuck out of my way, Maddox," I say, crushing my cell phone hard in my hand, hoping it'll temper the sting that Drew Montgomery's words inflicted on my heart. I push him to the side, caring less that I'm leaving him alone in my cubicle with all of my stuff and only about putting one foot in front of the other so I can succumb to the tears of having my heart broken in the peaceful haven of the ladies' room.

I'm vaguely aware that I hear Vincent's voice behind me, but I ignore it, knowing that if I turn around, I'll burst into tears or scream or throw that vase at his head.

1

LAUREN

I slam the empty shot glass that was previously filled with whiskey down on the mahogany bar and gesture towards the bartender that I may have been halfway interested in if I were just a little bit further in my grieving process. I don't know that I'm ready for no strings rebound sex yet. I'm still in phase one. Wallow in self-pity. Some self-loathing. Stare at pictures of me and Drew until I'm ready to throw up. Meaningless sex with a stranger doesn't usually happen until phase three.

The bartender refills my shot and cocks his head to the side, giving me a smile and a small nod as if to say *I get it* before heading over to the blonde at the end of the bar who is wearing a shirt that clearly shows she's going braless every time the door opened. I contemplate calling Charley, but then I remember the reason I didn't immediately call her and I'm instantly flooded with guilt. Charley is in wedding mode and is consistently in a full-fledged panic. She is getting her happily ever after, but that comes at the price of her sanity and an overbearing future mother-in-law.

I'd left my best friend just as the storm of her life slowly began to calm. A messy divorce involving an affair with her marriage counselor and a scorned husband that appeared not to want to let her go without a fight and an act of vengeance. It took a long year for Charley and Will to get to where they are now, blissfully happy with the most gorgeous baby girl and their nuptials coming up in just a few short months.

My blood runs cold at the thought.

Fuck. Now I have to see Drew and his new girlfriend there?

I huff indignantly before downing another shot.

A gust of cold air hits my back as the door opens behind me and, instantly, I shiver. It's times like this I desperately miss Atlanta. Chicago only knows two temperatures, cold and colder except for the two weeks in June where it dances around seventy degrees. I miss spending days by the pool, and the perfect sun kissed tan that turned my naturally olive skin even darker. I let out a breath as my fourth shot in an hour hovers near my lips just as someone sits down directly next to me.

I am so not in the fucking mood for chit-chat.

"A shot of Jameson and whatever the Princess has been sucking down like a wasted girl at a frat party." He points at the bartender before tapping my shoulder once.

My eyes snap angrily to the man who clearly is not reading my 'fuck off' signals and I'm met with smug baby blues. "Excuse me? Why are you here?"

"Are you having an existential crisis? Is that what this is? Like *why are any of us here* type thing? Because... you should probably lay off the booze." He taps the rim of the shot glass that I'm still holding. Some of it sloshes over the side and I glare at him as whiskey coats my fingertips. I set it down before sliding my fingers through my lips to suck off the remaining liquid. I'm so irritated by this interaction I almost miss the look in his eyes as he watches my finger disappear between my lips. *Almost.*

"Here. In this bar. Breathing my air," I grit out.

"I saw you come in here an hour ago, and after you were blubbering in your office today, I figured I should check on you before you're carried out in a body bag."

"Charming." I nod.

He cocks his head to the side and for a fleeting moment, I see genuine concern in his eyes and then something else as he rakes his gaze over me. "What's going on, Michaels?"

"Why do you care? We are not friends. We are barely acquaintances."

He shrugs. "I like being the first to know the office gossip. It makes for excellent leverage." He leans against the bar on one elbow, giving me a cocky grin, and if I didn't know any better, I'd say he's flirting with me. To be honest, if I were in a better frame of mind, and he was literally anyone else on Earth—with the exception of someone that shared my DNA—I *might* respond to said flirting.

"You're a fucking tool."

"So, I've heard, but you're getting piss drunk forty-five feet from the station; you had to think there was a chance someone was going to see you."

"And it had to be you?"

"Right place, right time, I guess. I am a journalist, after all." He slides his gray pea coat off and sets it on the barstool next to us before settling in next to me. "We taking these shots or no?" He holds up his glass.

"I'm not toasting with you over anything except your resignation. Or them firing you. I'm not picky."

He doesn't say anything; he just roams his ocean colored eyes over me. Eyes that have a hint of playfulness behind them before tapping his glass with mine and downing the shot. He leans forward, letting his forearms rest on the bar. Forearms that are exposed after he rolled his sleeves to his elbows. A tattoo runs up his arm in black script I can't quite make out.

Fuck, I love a man with tattoos.

I take the shot, hoping that it'll knock this lustful feeling out of me, but if I know liquor, specifically whiskey, as well as I think I do, it'll only exacerbate the tingling sensation between my legs.

"Atta girl. Now you going to spill it?"

"I still don't know why you care so much and if it's just for gossip, then you'll be pretty disappointed, it's not really something the station will care about reporting."

He shrugs. "Well… maybe I care. Is that so hard to believe?" I stare at him unblinking.

He…cares? Did I read this situation with him all wrong?

"I mean you're not a worthy opponent when you're all emotional." He waves over me. "It's more fun to crush you when you're giving it your all."

"I'm out of here." I angrily throw some cash on the bar to cover my drinks and a plate of nachos I didn't even touch.

"Wait wait wait." He chuckles and grabs me by the elbow, his fingers curling around me and pulling with enough force to stop me in my tracks. "I was kidding, Michaels. God, I had no idea you had a sensitive side. Who would have thought the Ice Queen had feelings?"

"I'm far from cold. You just bring out the best of me, I guess." I flash him a smile that most men can't resist, revealing my perfectly straight teeth and flutter my eyelashes.

Evidently, Vince can't resist it either because his eyes flit to my mouth and trace my lips in that slow way I'd put on lipstick. "You had braces?"

I scrunch my nose and shake my head slowly. "No."

"You were born with…those?" He points at my mouth and I bite down on my bottom lip, revealing my top teeth again. I nod and he looks me up and down again.

He chuckles and I watch as his eyes roll in a circle. "It's a shame God made Satan so perfect."

I sink to the stool again and slap his arm, not quite playful, but not hard. *"I'm* Satan? Wow, glass houses, Maddox."

He chuckles and holds his finger up towards the bartender to ask for another shot. "Are the nachos trash?" He points to the untouched plate of cheesy chips and I shake my head.

"Not hungry."

"Perfect, because I am," he says before shoveling a chip piled with chicken, cheese, pico and guacamole in his mouth. "Can I get an order of buffalo wings and a Macallan neat?" The bartender moves away before shooting me a look in question. I shake my head letting him know I don't want anything.

I let out a sigh, knowing that Vincent Maddox is relentless in his quest for information and he isn't going to let this go. Who knows, maybe he'll have some male insight.

They're both fucking assholes, after all.

"Drew, my boyfriend…he broke up with me…" My voice breaks slightly, until something registers in my brain for the first time. "Hold the phone," I say putting a hand up towards him. "Did you call me…*perfect?"*

"Well, that was before you let that douchebag that was never good enough for you in the first place dump you. Now, I'm wondering what's wrong with you." His hand finds his chin and he taps it methodically. "You don't give head or something?"

My teeth snap together so hard, I briefly wonder if I've cracked a tooth. "Fuck off," I grit out.

"So…that's a yes, but you don't do it well."

I want to snap back, but I briefly wonder if Drew really was bored with our sex life. I shrug in defeat and stare at the shot I still haven't taken. "Maybe you're right. He left me for someone else." The silence stretches between us and I'm taking that to mean that the asshole actually feels bad. "He was supposed to move here."

"I know. You mentioned it in passing, and when you brought him to that gala a few months ago, he said it as well. I'm actually surprised he let you move here by yourself in the first place."

"Excuse me? *Let* me?" I snap, daring him to continue down this road of patriarchal bullshit.

"Calm down, Gloria Steinem." He rolls his eyes. "I'm just saying I'm surprised he didn't want to come right away to be with you and support you. You guys seemed pretty serious. Not to mention, I've heard rumblings that you were going to get engaged this year." I frown, wondering why he knew that, or more importantly, why he even cared, but I put the thought aside to unpack later.

"I wanted to get acclimated."

"Hmmm." He rubs his jaw, the sound of his hand

rubbing against his beard resonating in my veins. "Well, I've learned that absence makes the heart grow yonder *not* fonder. And distance at our age…" He shrugs, as if the answer is so easy and I'm stupid not to have figured it out sooner. "We're busy as fuck, Michaels. We're hustling our way to the top; no one has time to be checking in on a significant other three states and a time zone away. We want someone we can talk to when we get home from work. You know…to break up the fucking?"

I can't help the chuckle that escapes my lips. I'll admit the no fucking thing had been…*difficult.* A morbid thought floats through my mind that perhaps Drew hadn't been in the same boat regarding that.

Had he fucked that girl yet? Or did he wait until the second he sent that bullshit text before sticking his dick in her?

I open said text *because again, masochism,* briefly forgetting that Vince is sitting next to me. I read over the words when I hear a groan next to me.

"And via text no less? Jesus, Lauren." He runs a hand through his dirty blonde hair and his blue eyes narrow further as he plucks my phone from my hand. I try to grab it back but he holds a hand up keeping me away. "Good, you haven't responded. May I?"

"No!" I say reaching for my phone again.

"Did you talk to him? Did you call him after he sent this?" I hear the scolding in his voice and I'm shocked at the fact that it doesn't irritate me.

"No, I wasn't sure what to say. And I guess a part of me figured...until I respond it's not over." As I speak the words, as I hear them back, I hear how pathetic I sound, and I know Vince won't miss the opportunity to call me out for it. I cringe, awaiting the dig when I meet his eyes that seem filled with anything but criticism.

"He fell for someone else, Lauren. It's over, babe." He grabs another chip, dragging it through the river of cheese on the plate. "I see he took the coward's way out though, which means he's an even bigger douche than I thought." He sets my phone down on the bar before taking a sip of his drink.

"Well, one will always recognize another," I quip and he throws his head back as a hearty laugh leaves his lips.

"There she is." He shoots me a wink before taking another sip of his drink. His arm brushes against mine and heat floods my veins at the minor touch.

I'm getting drunker by the minute and my inhibitions are disappearing by the second. I lick my lips, as I prepare to open Pandora's box. "How come you don't have a girlfriend?"

He raises one eyebrow. "Who says I don't?" I pause, not sure how to respond when he laughs. "I don't. That's not to say I don't have a quality rotation for when I want to have fun, but no one I'm committing to." He takes a sip of his drink but his eyes never leave mine as he swallows.

"A *ho-tation?* God, you really are a cliché."

A cocky grin finds his face, one side quirking higher than the other. "Why do you care?"

"I don't." I flip some hair over my shoulder before pulling my long tresses over one side and exposing my neck to him. It's one of my signature moves when I'm trying to disarm a man. But why do I want to disarm *this* man all of a sudden?

"You sure about that?" I feel his eyes on the side of my face, tracing my throat and I feel the tension crackle slightly between us.

"Sure, about what?" I swirl my straw around my drink.

He leans forward and the smell of his cologne and the whiskey waft around me and spark an aphrodisiac I can't ignore. "That you don't care."

I turn my head to meet his penetrating gaze. His blue eyes are dark and I can't help but notice the traces of silver running through them. I feel my cheeks heating at the intensity of our stare off and I turn my head towards my shot. "I…don't."

"Mmmhmmm." He pulls away and I let out a breath I didn't realize I'd been holding. "Maybe I fuck other women because the one I want is unavailable."

"Unrequited love, huh? How tragic." I don't try to hide the sarcasm in my voice though I am wondering what woman potentially has Vincent Maddox tied up in knots.

"I'm not about to lose sleep over it. But I've wanted her for months and she refused to dump her boyfriend, and I mean...a guy's gotta eat." He smirks, running his tongue over his bottom lip and I hear the message loud and clear.

I scrunch my nose at his metaphor. "You're disgusting."

"If you think that's disgusting, clearly he didn't eat your pussy right either. God, you two were a pair." He unbuttons the top button on his shirt, revealing a dusting of chest hair and I briefly wonder what it would be like to run my fingers through it. What it would be like to run my fingers down his chest to see how far down the hair went.

I blink my eyes several times, trying to calm my racing heart and the pounding in my clit that came from Vincent Maddox uttering the word "pussy." *Particularly in reference to mine.*

"Are you just like not worried at all that I'll go to HR with all of your wildly inappropriate comments?"

"So, I can't say the word pussy while we are drinking at a bar but you can threaten me with bodily harm on the work premises? And honestly, I've never pegged you for a snitch; especially after all of the colorful names you've called me the last few months."

"You've deserved every one."

"Probably."

I take a long sip of my drink, hoping the icy liquid will cool the fire burning beneath my skin. I hate that he has this effect on me all of a sudden. Is this all just fueled by alcohol? Or has all of our back and forth over the past few months just been foreplay to get us to this moment when I finally broke up with Drew

Wait. A. Fucking. Minute.

I feel a finger skim mine gently and lips dangerously close to my ear. "Tell me what you're thinking about. You're making that face you make when you're concentrating hard on something."

I take a deep breath wondering what speaking these words aloud could potentially mean. "You said…" I clear my throat and tuck a hair behind my ear, allowing the alcohol to give me the courage to get this sentence out. "I mean…I'm not the woman…am I? The one that refused to dump her boyfriend?"

I turn my head to face him and bump his nose in the process, making our faces less than an inch apart. My vision is starting to blur slightly and I have the sinking feeling in my gut that I just embarrassed myself by revealing my hypothesis.

"You think all this time…I've wanted *you?*" He chuckles and I can feel my cheeks heating in humiliation.

I clear my throat and hop from the barstool, my legs wobbling slightly at the sudden change. "A simple no would have sufficed." I bite my bottom lip before snatching my purse from the bar and fleeing for the bathroom for the second time today after an interaction with Vincent Maddox.

God, I fucking hate him.

2

LAUREN

The ladies' room is a one stall and I'm grateful for the privacy as I push my way inside and slam my purse down before staring at my reflection. My mascara has run from the crying I did earlier and has dried slightly beneath my eyes. My cheeks are red from all the emotions I've been feeling the past few hours and my bottom lip is swollen from my sinking my teeth into the flesh. I don't look like a total train wreck but I've certainly looked better.

A knock on the door interrupts my thoughts and I look towards the door in annoyance at not being granted just one minute of peace today. "Just a second."

The knocking accelerates, the staccato beats getting more aggressive with each pound. "What the fuck?" I growl as I swing the door open and I'm met with Vincent Maddox peering down at me before he's *inside* the bathroom pushing me *hard* against the wall.

"What do you think you're— "I start when his hand finds my mouth.

"Shut. The. Fuck. Up. You've been a royal pain in my ass for fucking months, you know that Michaels?" I huff behind his hand and open my mouth slightly preparing to bite his palm but he pulls back before I can sink my teeth into the flesh. He leans forward, the smell of his cologne, his whiskey and the spearmint gum he's chewing all sink into my skin. "You think you're the woman I mentioned? That you're the object of this "unrequited love" you speak of? News flash, Princess. You're not. You're a neurotic know-it-all that's done nothing but make my life hell since you flew in on your broomstick," he sneers.

"Fuck— "

"However," he cuts me off and taps my nose, and despite my aggravation, I'm curious to hear what's following that qualifier, "I've been fantasizing about pinning you to the conference room table and feeding you my cock until your cunt creams all over it since the first time I saw you from behind in that black pencil skirt. I've spent more time than I care to admit wondering what your pussy would feel like wrapped around my cock. What it would feel like under my tongue when I make you orgasm." His hands have found their way to either side of my head as he leans down and speaks so close to my mouth I wonder if he's going to kiss me.

To be honest I think I would let him.

"I've almost broken my dick off thinking about you riding my cock as your fucking tits bounce. And what your smart-ass mouth would feel like wrapped around my cock. I want you, Lauren Michaels, but in no way, shape, or form am I in love with you."

My mouth drops open at his sinful monologue. Under normal circumstances, I would have a comeback ready and waiting the second he referred to me as a witch. But I'm drunk. I'm also in a very enclosed space with quite frankly one of the sexiest men I've ever met. Even if he is also the most infuriating, my level of intoxication is allowing me to overlook that. Especially since said sexy man is talking about putting his mouth on my pussy which is currently pulsing faster with each passing second.

My conscience barely has a chance to scream *bad idea, abort mission* before my lips are on his. My tongue pushes through his lips at the exact second his hands find their way into my hair. I told myself I wasn't ready for this yet, but there is something about this man that makes me want to think with my hormones instead of my head. *Or my heart.* "Just sex. Just this once." I let out a sigh as one hand drops from my hair and moves under my skirt and presses against my heated core.

"Fuck. Done." He growls just before he bites down on my bottom lip. "But I want it all." His tongue soothes the sting of his bite before moving down my neck and sucking at the skin just behind my ear.

"Define all," I whimper.

"You know what the fuck I mean, Michaels. I want your mouth, your pussy, and your sexy little ass." He tells me as he lifts me into his arms and pins me to the wall. My legs immediately wrap around him and I'm dizzy with more than just too much whiskey. His dick is stabbing my pussy and with each thrust I'm getting closer and closer to the edge.

"I don't agree to those terms," I snap knowing there's no way I'm letting him stick his cock in my ass.

"Why? No room with the stick that's lodged in there?" His fingertips dig into my ass cheeks as he continues to pound against me at a relentless speed. His forehead drops to my shoulder and he groans against my neck. "I'm going to come in my pants dry humping you in a bathroom like a fucking teenager at prom." His thrusts become erratic and his breathing speeds up.

"Would you rather come on my tongue?"

And here comes bold Lauren. Sexy Lauren. Nasty Lauren.

He stops and pulls back slowly. His eyes dancing wildly with lust and surprise. He sets me to my feet and drops his pants in seconds, and I'm on my knees just as fast, sheathing my mouth around quite frankly one of the prettiest dicks I've ever seen in my life. I've never been with a man that manscaped; I am used to a thrush of wild and untamed pubic hair, not the neat trim around a man's shaft.

A loud guttural moan fills the stall and I know if

anyone is waiting on the other side, they are well aware of what's happening inside these four walls. A hand finds my hair pulling it into a ponytail on the top of my head as he thrusts into my eager mouth. "I need to see your face," he growls. "Look at me, Michaels." I look up at him and the second my green eyes find his, I'm lost. "God, you're so fucking pretty." He chokes out and it's as if his words stoke the fire between my legs because my clit tingles almost painfully. My hand moves between my legs and into my panties, desperate for any bit of relief.

"If you think I'm going to let you come anywhere but, on my tongue, the first time, you've lost your fucking mind. Don't touch your pussy, Lauren."

"But…"

"Do. Not. Touch. Your. Pussy," he commands, his cock pushing to the back of my throat with each word. I listen because I've read *Fifty Shades of Grey* one too many times, so I'm pretty much conditioned to respond to any level of dominance. I slide my hand from between my legs as I continue to suck his cock. I wrap a hand, the same hand that was just between my legs around the base of his shaft and begin sucking him faster.

"I want to paint your face with my cum," he growls and a part of me wants to tell him absolutely not. That he's lost his mind if he thinks I'll let him degrade me that way. But another part, a smaller yet louder part wants to tell him he can come anywhere he wants. That

I want the degradation. I don't feel humiliated, I feel empowered.

"Not here." I pull him out and circle the head with my tongue before sliding my mouth back down his cock.

"Fuck. You suck cock like a pornstar." He pulls again and the prickle in my scalp sends a spark to my sex.

"Stop talking and fucking come already."

"Watch your mouth, Michaels." He pulls my hair again.

"The mouth wrapped around your dick right now? You should watch yours unless you want to feel my teeth, Maddox." I grit out and his cock twitches in response. "Oh really?"

"Your sassy ass mouth turns me on, Lauren. Stop talking and suck." He thrusts again, pushing himself further into my mouth. He hits the back of my throat and I choke slightly. "Fuck, that feels good." *Yeah, I'll bet.*

I slowly move back down his dick, my hands finding his balls, massaging them gently and tugging slightly every few seconds. I press my finger to his perineum and he gasps and sputters in response. "Holy fucking shit. I'm going to come. Tell me you swallow."

I meet his gaze and he mouths *thank you God* when he sees the look I'm giving him, and then he comes long and hard down my throat. He comes so much, my mouth fills with the liquid faster than I can get it down my throat causing my cheeks to puff out and he smiles in response. "Swallow."

I do as he says, sucking it down slowly so I don't choke. Once I'm finished, he pulls me to my feet and presses his lips to mine. His tongue invades my mouth and he groans—assumedly at tasting himself—and I'm briefly turned on at this man's level of masculinity. Drew hated kissing me after I'd gone down on him and I always found that kind of strange that he'd be willing to kill the moment over something so minor.

His hands cup my cheeks as he continues to make love to my mouth, rubbing his tongue languidly against mine. "Come home with me," he whispers against my mouth. It's not a question, but a command, almost a plea.

I nod without a second thought.

3

LAUREN

T he ride home is quite frankly not my finest moment, and I'm grateful that Vince called the Uber because we definitely tanked his rating. The second we climb into the backseat I'm in his lap grinding against him like a stripper at a bachelor party and we don't come up for air until the driver slams on his brakes and not so politely tells us to "get the fuck out."

The second we are out of the Uber a giggle leaves my lips. "He didn't like us too much."

"I'll live." He pulls me, not only into his arms but over his shoulder. I squeal in response and he slaps my ass before groping it hard. "Jesus Christ, your ass Lauren." His hands move down my legs to my ankles and he squeezes. "I'm going to fuck you with these sexy heels on." I smile, thinking about how these particular shoes make me feel. They're nude Valentino rock stud heels; I'd bought them with my first big girl paycheck and they always make me feel like a badass woman that can take on anything. It doesn't hurt that they make my legs look a mile long either.

He gets us through the entrance to his building and I look around my surroundings as he walks. The lobby is spacious and smells of lavender. Gray suede couches are scattered throughout and there's a large television mounted on the wall. A fireplace crackles in the corner that gets quieter as we move towards the elevators.

"Let me down!" I squeal and he does the second the elevators close and we begin to ascend to what appears to be the top floor.

"You're so fucking sexy," he tells me as he presses his lips to mine again. "I can't wait to spank this pretty little ass of yours and then eat it." He grabs my ass for good measure and I gasp in response.

"What's this obsession you have with my ass?"

"I'm an ass man and yours is phenomenal."

The elevator dings and then we are moving towards his door. Within moments we are inside his apartment and the door has barely closed before he's on his knees in front of me.

"I need a taste and I can't wait another second." He yanks my pencil skirt up around my waist and groans when he sees what's underneath. I mentally praise myself for choosing to wear thigh highs today, specifically ones attached to a garter belt. "Holy fucking shit." He unclips it from my stockings and removes it letting it fall to the floor. At this point, my white satin panties are beyond soaked and I'm dying for any type of relief. He slides them down slowly and I step out of them, careful not to let my heels snag them. For a second, no one says anything and I watch as Vince stares at my cunt like he's never seen one before.

"What's wrong? Why are you just…looking at me?"

He licks his lips before looking up at me, his blue eyes dark and sinful. "I'm trying to figure out how one night with you will ever be enough," he tells me in what I think to be a rare moment of drunk vulnerability. He spreads my sex exposing my throbbing clit to his mouth and just when I think he's going to press his tongue to where I need it most he blows gently.

"Fuck, Vince!" I scream and he groans in response to my outburst. His tongue is rough and yet it feels like silk as he rubs it back and forth across my clit. He grabs my right leg and slides it over his shoulder, opening me up to him. The cool air hits my sex and I clench at the raw sexiness of the situation.

Vincent Maddox on his knees.

In front of me.

Eating my pussy.

"Fuck." I groan the second he attaches his mouth to my swollen clit. "Oh my God." My hand moves through his silky dark blonde hair as he works me over. Sliding his tongue inside of me before moving back upwards to suck on my clit. He rolls his tongue around it before pulling it between his teeth and just as my knees begin to buckle, he nibbles gently.

Fuck. How does he know I love that?

My eyes flutter shut, and I feel them roll back even behind my lids. My toes curl inside my pumps and I curse myself for not removing them first because the second the orgasm passes, I'll feel the discomfort of how hard my toes are curled. But right now, I couldn't care if every bone in all my toes shattered. "Oh God, don't stop. I think I'm going to come." I push him harder against me, desperate for the feeling of euphoria that only this sexy act can bring. I look down just in time for him to slow his ministrations and take one slow lick through my sex. *And then again. And again. And again.*

My clit is throbbing almost painfully, and I'm seconds from passing out from the pleasure. "Vince, oh my God, there!" I scream as I move my hips in time with his lips, rolling them against his face as the orgasm explodes from me. I barely have a second to come down from the high or slow my racing heart before I'm lifted into his arms and his lips are on mine. I don't know how many steps it is or how long we are on the move. The only thing I'm aware of is the feeling between my legs and the softest lips kissing mine and then I'm lowered onto a plush bed with the softest sheets I've ever felt.

"I love the taste of your pussy," he tells me as he pulls off his clothes at record speed. I follow suit, sliding my skirt down and pulling my sweater over my head. I reach around my back to unclasp my bra when I feel him pulling my cup down to release my nipple. I don't have a chance to unclasp it before I feel something cool against my skin and then a loud *rip.* My eyes fly open to meet his and the lust crackles between us, but it immediately switches to annoyance when I see the small blade in his hand. I look down and see that my brand new La Perla bra has been cut in half between my breasts.

"Are you *insane?*" I growl at him. "This bra is fucking expensive you asshole." He doesn't respond, he just tosses his knife somewhere out of sight. "And what the fuck are you even doing with a knife?"

Well, you do live in Chicago, Lo. It's why your brother-in-law insists you carry pepper spray.

He doesn't answer, he just circles my nipple with his tongue and sucks it into his mouth before biting down gently. "You're buying me a new one," I mumble under my breath and he bites down harder. I gasp in response.

"Stop talking about the fucking bra and let me fuck you already." He bites again and I moan under his touch. He lets me go with a pop, before his fingers find it, rolling it between his fingers. They dance up my chest, stroking the sensitive skin on my neck towards my lips. "Suck," he growls before sliding his index and middle finger in my mouth. I do as he asks, swirling my tongue around them, as the last bit of annoyance floats away. He slides them out and then his fingers are between my legs, stroking the sensitive space there. "Fuck, you're so ready for me." He pauses when he pulls out and looks down at me, cock in hand as he drags it through my cunt once. "I want to fuck you bare so bad."

"No," I tell him. I'm horny but I'm not stupid, and I am on good authority to report that I'm not the only girl he's fucked in our office, and who knows how many else outside of it.

He seems to be surprised by my firmness but nods once. I hear him shuffling next to his bedside table, revealing a condom and rolling it on. "Get on your hands and knees." He orders and I comply immediately. Getting fucked from behind is my favorite position and I'm eager to feel his cock so deep inside me like only this position can provide. I've barely settled when he slams into me with a series of expletives. "Holy fuck, you're tight," he groans just as his hand comes down *hard* on my ass.

"Oh my God," I cry out before dropping my head to the bed. I bite down on the pillow in front of me as he continues to pound into me at a relentless speed.

"Fuck. I did not want to come this fast," he says and I can tell he's gritting his teeth. I clamp down on him, my muscles squeezing him as hard as I can and his hand finds my ass again. "Don't fucking do that."

"Why?" I breathe out. I know it'll only take one swipe of my fingers over my clit for me to detonate beneath him but part of me wants to make him work for it. "I'm c—close, Vince," I manage to stammer out between the deep breaths I'm trying to get into my lungs. My eyes flutter shut as I clutch the sheets beneath us, my body climbing higher and higher with every thrust. I feel his hands in my hair, pulling just hard enough to make my scalp tingle as he fucks me harder. The familiar feeling in my sex begins and just as his pumps become more uncontrolled, I come *hard.* "Fuck fuck fuck!" I cry out as my body succumbs to the most intense orgasm of my life. I squeeze my eyes shut just as he comes, pressing his cock as far inside as he can go.

"Holy fuck." I feel what I assume to be a bead of sweat drop to my back and then his tongue, trailing up my spine. I shiver as he pulls out, the loss of his body heat chilling me instantly. He falls to his back and I turn my head towards him to find him staring at the ceiling.

"I knew you'd be a good fuck."

"How do you make a compliment sound offensive?"

"It's a skill. Want a beer or water or anything?"

"I'm good, and I should probably go," I say as I begin to climb out of bed. He grabs my arm, holding me in place.

"We said one night and as far as I'm concerned the night isn't over yet."

THE FEELING OF AN ACTUAL POUNDING BEHIND MY EYES, followed by a wave of nausea, and the desperate need to chug a gallon of water has my eyes flying open, waking me from the last few moments of sleep. I groan at the light streaming through the curtains and press a hand to my eyes, turning into the pillow. I swallow, trying to create moisture in my dry mouth, and the flavors lingering there transport me back to the night before.

Whiskey and Vincent Maddox's cum.

I shoot up in bed as my mind is finally catching up with the fact that not only am I not at my sister's house where I have taken up residence the last few months, but I'm still at Vince's.

Naked.

In his bed.

The events of the day before come rushing back to me and my heart begins to pound in my chest.

I fucked Vince, the biggest asshole in Chicago.

Oh my God.

"Morning, Princess," I hear from the doorway and my head snaps to the side to see Vincent walking towards me with a cup of coffee in his hands. His sweatpants hang low on his hips showcasing that delicious V that I became well acquainted with last night. I rake my eyes up his bare torso and meet his, less ashamed than I should have been to have been caught ogling him.

Despite my staring, I hold the sheet up around my chest to try and maintain a modicum of modesty now that we were no longer under the darkness of night and a bottle of whiskey. "Nothing I haven't seen before." He points at me before sitting next to me. "You want me to call you an Uber or you want—" He starts and I hold a hand up in response not really interested in hearing how he's going to try and blow me off. I'm not like the normal girls he fucks. I don't want breakfast, or morning sex, or hell, even a kiss goodbye. I want to get the fuck out of here and never speak of last night again.

"I'm good, I'll get my own," I tell him as I sit up, snatching my panties and ruined bra off the floor. I run my finger over the blue satin, my lips forming a pout at the limited edition set that was a gift from Drew.

Out with the old, I guess.

"I can't believe you ruined this," I mutter before pulling my blouse over my bare breasts.

"Listen… Michaels." He looks me over as I hop off the bed and pull my skirt up my legs. Surprisingly, he looks away. "I'd appreciate if we could keep this between us."

I look at him for a beat, wondering how he could possibly think I'd want to reveal to anyone that I sold my soul to the devil for a few good orgasms.

Okay, great orgasms. Spectacular even. Orgasms so good at one point I could have sworn I saw God.

"I wasn't planning to, but why don't you want people to know?" I raise an eyebrow at him. "What are you embarrassed of me or something? Because I'm way out of *your* league," I sneer. I'm hungover and the awkwardness of my current situation is making me feel a little petty.

He snorts and gets up without another glance. "Right, Michaels. I'm sorry, didn't *you* just get dumped?"

"Wow. Asshole," I snap before grabbing my coat from the floor and sliding it on.

"But you saying you're out of my league is…"

"For one, the truth," I say holding up a finger. "And two I only uttered said truth because you were acting like you were embarrassed."

He takes a step closer to me and I take a step back. We do this a few more times until I'm against the wall and he's towering over me. "Alright, clearly your ego is a little bruised after yesterday, so I'll give you this *one*. I'm not embarrassed that I fucked you, Michaels. You're hot, and you know you're hot. You may even be the hottest girl at the office, depending on the day and what that hot blonde in sales is wearing. But I don't want you swooning or staring at me with hearts in your eyes just because I made you come…*a lot*." He smirks and I scowl at his comment. "We had sex once, I don't see why things have to change at the office, that's all."

"Fine by me." I push him slightly to get him out of my space. "I'm leaving." I don't wait for his response before I'm out of his bedroom and scurrying through his living room to his front door. I'm barely out the door when I slap a hand over my mouth and let out a muffled scream.

Fuck.

How could I have rebounded with Vincent Maddox?

4

LAUREN

"Maddox, Michaels, get in here," I hear from my cubicle, and I'm immediately on edge hearing mine and Vince's name spoken in the same sentence.

I'm still nursing the worst hangover I've had since college and I've been able to avoid Vince ever since I got here. I slide my pumps on that I'd kicked off the second I sat down at my desk before making my way to my boss' office.

Vincent is already seated when I get there and I reluctantly take the seat next to him. I slide the chair a few inches away from him to try and put some space between us, but evidently, I'm not all that sly because my boss stares at me over his glasses.

Jack Owens is a no-nonsense kind of boss that doesn't take anyone's bullshit. Sometimes he'd put up with mine, but that was only after I'd nailed a story. He pulls his glasses off and slides them across his desk.

"Enough. Both of you." I frown, a blush finding my cheeks as I prepare to be chastised. "I'm sick of both of your shit. My kids act more mature than both of you. If I didn't know any fucking better, I'd say you were in love with each other."

I choke on seemingly nothing and stare at him with wide eyes. "False. Fake news." I cross my arms and glower at my boss. He raises an eyebrow at my boldness though he's come to expect it before shaking his head.

He runs his fingertips over his graying goatee before pointing at both of us. "Be that as it may, I'm assigning you both to a story."

"Together?" Vince and I say at the same time.

"Yes, together." He nods.

"Why? I can handle it alone." Vince says and I snap my head towards him.

"Yes, me too." I nod my head vigorously, my ponytail tapping my shoulders with each shake. My head throbs slightly, reminding me that I really shouldn't be making too many sudden movements in my condition.

"You're doing it together because, quite frankly, I'm sick of the back and forth between you two and since you're insistent on acting like children, I'm going to treat you like it. You're co-writing this story. It's a fluff piece more or less, but this woman is gaining traction on Twitter and I want a piece on it by the end of the weekend. You two are quick; it shouldn't take much time out of your scheduled fighting."

I let out a sigh, already admitting defeat that I'm going to be spending the weekend arguing about syntax with fucking Vincent Maddox. "What is it?"

He taps his top lip before he slides a stack of papers across his desk. I frown when I note the tweets. "She's… a psychic?"

Vince snorts next to me before standing and running a hand through his hair. I try to ignore the flash of pulling on that luscious head of hair while he sucked at the wet flesh between my legs but it's no use and I feel my cheeks starting to heat slightly. "My talents are clearly needed elsewhere; Lauren can handle it."

"I didn't realize I phrased that as a question." Jack stares up at Vince before lowering his gaze back to the chair as if to say 'sit the fuck down.' "If I did, I apologize, but this isn't a request. You're doing this."

I note him lowering back to his seat in my periphery as my eyes scan over the thousands of tweets and retweets and shares about the woman who lived in a rundown shack a few towns over and had been predicting essentially everything over the past few months and even helped the police locate a few dead bodies.

Creepy as fuck.

"So, what, she can talk to the dead? Is she like a medium?" I ask, my apprehensive eyes finding my boss'.

I'm not sure I believe in ghosts or any of that but I'm not so sure I don't believe in them either.

"How the hell should I know? That's why I want an interview. I want her story and I want you two to report on it."

I look down at the sheets he'd printed from a bunch of accounts as well as a few vague articles regarding the police investigations.

"We aren't crime reporters," Vince speaks up as he reads over my shoulder.

I try to shuffle away from him because his cologne is distracting as hell, but he leans in closer when I try to move.

"Then don't talk about the crime part. Our social media has been a snooze lately and I want to shake things up."

"And you think Miss Cleo here will help?" Vince snorts. "Psychics are bullshit, I'd bet five hundred bucks she's full of shit and she probably had something to do with said dead bodies."

My head snaps to his, my mind racing at the thought that this woman could be potentially dangerous. "You think?"

"You really think she just knew where the bodies were buried? And she called a few winning lottery tickets, big fucking deal." Vince shrugs.

"Just go meet her and stop arguing with me before I make you work this weekend," Jack snaps before putting his Air Pods back in, effectively dismissing us.

I WALK OUT OF THE OFFICE BEHIND VINCE BECAUSE HE was raised by wolves and thus has no manners. "Let's get this shit over with. I have tickets to the Bulls game tonight. We can take my car." He follows me back to my cubicle so that I can grab my computer and a few things I'll need for the interview.

"Awesome because I don't have a car."

He leans up against my makeshift wall and cocks his head to the side in question. "Why? Are you like…poor?"

"No, fuckwit. Because I don't *need* a car. I live fifteen minutes from here and the CTA and Ubers do just fine. I sold my car…a really nice car, mind you, when I left Atlanta and I just haven't needed one since I got here."

He raises an eyebrow at me. "Don't you live at your sister's house?"

"Again, because she has the space and I haven't fully committed to staying in Chicago. I didn't want to commit to a lease just to leave in six months to go back to Atlanta. Besides, I moved here in part to be closer to my niece. Living in the same house with her is about as close as I can get. Any other questions?"

That seems to shut him up and we fall in step as we walk towards his office. An office that Jack had tried to get us to share when I transferred here, but neither of us would hear of it. I am perfectly fine with my cubicle that is out of the way where no one really bothers me. Well, except Vince.

"How old is she?" he asks and I don't even try to hide the shock that he's asking me a question about myself.

"Five. Her name is Emma."

"Cute. She's probably got you wrapped around her finger, huh?" He grabs his laptop and his charger before sliding it into a messenger bag. He grabs a half-eaten protein bar I see on his desk before tidying up the few papers that are scattered on top. His office is organized and smells of his cologne and paper. Fresh crisp paper straight out of the printer. The smell makes something inside me whirl to life. I'm not just turned on sexually, but mentally. My eyes dart to the diploma on his wall, Northwestern, and I note the accolade underneath: Summa Cumme Laude. *Damn, who knew he was actually smart? In like a bookish way, obviously.*

I've never really paid attention to anything in his office. The only time I come here is when we're arguing, and that usually ends with me slamming the door behind me and not exactly taking in my environment.

My eyes meet his again and I notice a grin on his face, like because I'm observing my surroundings it means I'm somehow interested in his life. I roll my eyes and move out of his office. "You ready? Let's just get this over with."

"Scarlett Stone. Forty-five years old. Native of New York. Came to Illinois seventeen years ago with her twin brother who later died of a nasty case of... staph infection?" I wrinkle my nose as Vincent drives down the Kennedy expressway. We're only a few exits from our destination and I'm trying to learn as much about our subject as possible before we get there.

"Oh, you've got to be fucking kidding me. He died from something he probably caught from a communal gym shower? Which by the way is very curable."

I ignore his outburst and continue reading. "It says she took his death hard, especially after escaping New York City just a few years prior. She said 'New York chewed up my parents and spit *us* out.'"

"Sounds dark."

"Says she's had a string of odd jobs up until about five years ago when she started the psychic business. Fortune telling, palm reading, reading tea leaves, et cetera." I let out a sigh because even I'm not sure I'm buying what she's selling.

"And *that* keeps her lights on? Yeah, I call bullshit."

"I'm just reading what's here, Vince."

"Well, I don't buy it."

"You can call her on it when you meet her."

"What the fuck kind of name is Scarlett Stone anyway? She sounds like she ripped the name off a seventies pornstar. What's her real name?"

I look through a few more of the papers, curious if

maybe Vince was right and Scarlett Stone was just an alias. "I don't see anything about a birth name."

He pulls off the exit and we spend the rest of the ride in silence. It isn't until what feels like fourteen different turns that we find ourselves in front of her alleged house. I was expecting something much creepier and more rundown, but the "shack" is actually just a small one-story house that isn't in terrible shape. I follow Vince down the path towards the front door, ignoring the leaves that haven't been raked or the weeds that are in desperate need of whacking.

"She needs a gardener."

"I doubt that's a luxury she can afford, Vince." I roll my eyes and knock on her front door.

"Who's there?" a voice calls from inside. It's higher pitched than I expected with an undeniable New York accent.

"Ummm, I'm Lauren Michaels, we uhh…work for NBC?"

"Not interested." Her voice has gone down several octaves, coming out more stern than before.

"We've heard all about you. We were hoping we could have our fortunes told? And maybe a palm reading?"

Vince coughs and shakes his head before whispering. "You've lost your mind if you think I'm going to pay this dingbat to hold my hand and tell me I have mommy issues and I hate my sister. But chin up, old sport, in New Year you'll keep your health and find wealth if you only believe in yourself," he says sarcastically.

"Mommy issues." I slap my forehead dramatically. "Of course. It all makes sense."

"Fuck off," he mouths and I give him my middle finger in response.

"It's forty for the palm read, sixty for both."

"Fuck that!" Vince whispers, though I'm sure the woman on the other side heard it loud and clear.

"And you called *me* poor earlier? Loosen the purse strings, Maddox."

He snorts. "This is bullshit."

"We need the story."

"Not for a hundred and twenty bucks."

"Fine, I'll just do it. But you're coming in just in case she tries to use me as a sacrifice to a demon."

"I'll let her take you," he mumbles under his breath just as the door opens.

I shoot him a glare before turning back to the woman at the door who can't be but a few inches over four feet tall. Round glasses sit in front of bright blue eyes and on top of a button nose. Her long graying hair is almost to her knees and she has it pulled back with a bandana. She's wearing a kimono, an actual kimono, with Ugg boots that look like they've been through hell and back.

Wow, she's like a caricature of a fortune teller.

She sizes us up and down the same way, probably noting my heels that I definitely should have changed and my cashmere coat as well as Vince's attire. "How far did you come to see me?"

"Uh…we're from Chicago, so not far."

"Hmmm…" She looks back and forth between Vince and me before turning and beckoning us with her finger over her shoulder. "Shoes off at the door."

"What? No thanks." Vince immediately argues as he closes the door behind us.

"I don't want you to track in anything from out there." She points.

"You really care about dirt?" Vince scoffs, and I'll admit even I'm surprised she's concerned about that as I take in the small living space that I would not describe as clean.

"I care about you tracking in evil."

Vince shoots me a look as I slide my heels off, wishing like hell I had worn socks because I'm not one hundred percent sure I won't catch tetanus from the flooring. I watch as Vince pulls off his dress shoes and sits them neatly next to mine before pulling off his socks as well. I'm about to ask why he's risking it when he hands them to me. I cock my head in shock, completely blown away by his gesture when he sighs. "Don't make a big deal out of it."

"Your socks?" A smile pulls at the corner of my lips and he rolls his eyes.

"Don't tell me you're weird about feet when you were literally sucking my balls while I had my tongue in your ass last night," he whispers.

My cheeks heat as he walks by me and towards a small table. I follow in tow after slipping his socks on, trying to ignore the blood singing in my veins after his comment. I sit next to him and watch as Scarlett moves around the room, collecting things off of shelves and setting them on the table. She stops and looks at me before pulling her glasses off and to the top of her head. "Anyone ever tell you, you look like that princess?" I nod, knowing who she means. "The one that married Princess Diana's son. Shame what happened to that one."

"Meghan Markle. Yes, I've heard it."

"Spitting image." She looks at Vince and shakes her head. "You look nothing like Harry though. This your beau?" She looks at me from over her glasses as she points at Vince.

I snap my head towards him and shake my head. "No, absolutely not."

"Really?" She sits down across from us. "You sure?"

"I'm very sure." I nod, and I feel my palms start to sweat at the idea of being questioned over my recent change in relationship with Vince.

"But you've had...relations. Recently?"

Fuck. "What? No...and that's not why we're here." I tell her.

"You said you wanted me to read your palm and tell your fortune. That's going to be all over there, sweetheart. Your aura gives you away."

I hear a chuckle next to me and she frowns. "Yours

does too, Casanova. You've been pining for this girl… sometimes you walk by her office just to catch a glimpse of her."

He freezes in his seat and I note that he shifts almost nervously? "Joke's on you, she doesn't have an office."

"Oh, I'm sorry…I don't know the term for it. It's a room, without four walls." She closes her eyes as if she's imagining it. "A ummm…like a cubby?"

"Cubicle," I whisper and she points at me.

"That." She closes her eyes again and holds her hand out towards Vince. "You left her flowers once…wait, no…a plant when hers died."

"That was you?" I ask in shock. I had been a little negligent in watering and making sure it got any light besides the fluorescent lighting in my office.

"No." He scoffs. "I mean…Jack's assistant picked up an extra and I told her to give it to you."

"Why didn't you tell me?" I bite my bottom lip as I hear the first nice thing, he's ever done for me…*last night aside.*

"So, you could look at me like that? I know your friend Charlotte gave you that plant when you left Atlanta and you were sad when it died. Let's not make it a thing."

"You just broke up with someone." She points at me and I snap my gaze away from Vince. "A guy that doesn't live here…"

"So, what, that makes you a psychic? I just said she

moved here from Atlanta," Vince argues and she ignores him and continues to stare at me.

"It starts with an A?" She speaks and I gasp.

"No, it doesn't." Vince snaps and I turn my gaze back to him, irritated.

"What do you think Drew is short for, you moron?"

His cheeks pinken slightly and he lowers his head. I wish I hadn't said his name because I was curious if Scarlett actually knew it. "He left you for someone else?" she asks, but it sounds more like a statement.

"That's the story," I whisper.

"Hmmm...it won't last. He'll be back, honey. They always come back."

"I'm not sure I want him back."

"Of course not, he's a Virgo. No good for a Pisces." She points at me. "You probably had some good kinky sex but it wasn't meant for long term. A Virgo- Pisces romance is like shooting stars, bright and intense but fizzle out quickly."

"How did you—" I start and shake my head, wondering if this woman really is the real deal.

"And you're a water sign...a Scorpio to be exact." She points at Vince. "This is probably why you have such chemistry. You two are highly compatible. Though, in your case, it seems more like opposites attract. Conflict turned passion. Tale as old as time with you two. You're moody and stubborn, possessive even." There's a gleam in her eye as she gestures towards Vince and then she smiles. "It's strange, though, should you marry you'll have to overcome your differences. Love-hate relationships can be strong at first but they can be exhausting in the long run."

"I'm sorry, when did we get married?" Vince asks.

"Hmmm, I see you two at a wedding. Not yours though. Well, maybe yours." She smirks but she shakes her head. "No, this is for someone else and soon…your friend." She points at me. "The one that gave you the plant?"

"Charley?"

"Yes, she's getting married…*again?*"

Holy shit!

"Ummm, yeah, next month."

"You're her date?" She asks Vince and he shoots a look at me before turning back to Scarlett.

"No?"

"Hmmm, interesting. There's still time though." She smiles before turning back to me. "So, you've only had sex the one time then?"

"Okay, this is not why we're here," Vince interjects before I can answer…and surprisingly I was going to answer. I'm curious to hear what she has to say about me and Vince. Even if I don't believe it, she does, and I want to know what she thinks she can see in us.

"She said she wanted your palm read."

"And you're not holding her palm!" he snaps.

"Fine, give me." She holds her hand out and I slide mine into hers and she turns it upwards, running her fingers over the skin. "So soft."

"Thank you?" I smile as she lowers her glasses over her eyes again. "Okay, you've got strong lines. See this here? This is your heart line, some people call it your love line, but different strokes for different readers." She points at me as she traces the line from the edge of my hand towards my index finger. Yours is long which I could have seen coming because hello, Pisces and also, you seem like a sweet girl. So, you see, your heart line ends here, right at the Mount of Jupiter which means you have an abundance of love to give but some high expectations."

"High maintenance, more like." Vince crosses his arms.

"It means she loves hard but doesn't take any shit." Scarlett's eyes snap to Vince and stares him down before turning back to me. "I hope he at least made you come, dear."

"Oh, she came alright," he mumbles and I kick him under the table.

"God, Vince, shut *up!*" I growl, causing Scarlett to snicker under her breath.

She goes on to read my life, head, marriage, and children lines telling me that I'm high energy, good at sports and vigorous activities, good at thinking, considerate of others, bold and exuberant, but I am easy to become 'a dragon lady.' I'm also predicted to have two marriages and all girls.

The rest of the visit is pretty similar to the beginning

with Vince questioning everything she says and Scarlett snapping back in the sassiest ways.

I kind of like her.

We do get some quality information about the bodies she helped discover and some of her other predictions but I can't stop fixating on what she predicted for me…and oddly enough the infuriating man next to me.

"Did you buy all that shit?" Vince asks the second the door closes behind us and we start down her walkway towards his car.

"She did know a lot. How else would she know we slept together?"

"Because you're staring at me with stars in your eyes?" He grins, pulling at his lips.

"I think you're confusing stars with a look of disgust, but okay, Vince." We walk down the path towards the car when I stop in my tracks. "She knew about the plant. And Drew and…that I'm going to Charley's wedding. Her *second* wedding."

"Yeah, about that, she's already on wedding number two? What's wrong with her? We're barely thirty."

"Nothing! And don't be a dick. Her first husband… Matt was…" I scrunch my nose trying to figure out the best way to explain my best friend's ex-husband. Matt was manipulative. He didn't want to be married. He cared more about his job than he did about her." The list is endless, but I'm not interested in getting into the gritty details with Vince.

"Hmmm." He leans over the car and stares at me. "Sounds like she's a little needy."

"Sounds like you're a little judgmental." I open his passenger door and climb in. When I look towards the house, my eyes tracing it from top to bottom, I note Scarlett at the window. She shoots me a wave and if I'm not mistaken, a wink.

5

LAUREN

"**Y**ou want to grab something to eat?" Vince's voice breaks the silence that we've been sitting in the past ten minutes as we drive back to the city.

"I thought you had tickets to the game?"

"Fuck." He presses his hand to his forehead. "I completely forgot. I've already canceled on her twice."

Her.

"Her? Like a girlfriend?"

"You jealous?" There's something in his voice I can't quite pinpoint. *Annoyance...or hope?*

"No, but circling back to your tongue in my ass thing? If you have a girlfriend, that makes you the worst." I cross my arms and stare at him, trying to convince my brain that I do *not* find him attractive despite what my hormones are saying.

He chuckles and shakes his head, and I'm instantly

furious for letting myself get involved with this narcissist. "Not a girlfriend. We have mutual friends. We went out once. It's casual."

"But you've fucked her?" The words spill out of my mouth like word vomit.

Fuck. I cannot be jealous. I cannot be feeling territorial over a guy that I fucked once and spent the last few months calling every name in the book.

"Who wants to know?"

"I'm just asking." I try to appear unfazed but I know everything about my body language reads differently.

"Well, since you and I were only a one-time thing, I don't think you're entitled to that information." His words are somewhat harsh, but I note his dimple popping out beneath his beard.

"So yes." I roll my eyes.

"She sucked my dick in the bathroom of this club. That's it." He shrugs.

I try to ignore the annoyance over this piece of information bubbling in my gut but it's no use and I can feel myself shutting down by the second. "So, you're *that* guy? The one who gets off hooking up with women in clubs and…bars?" I shoot him a side eye and he rolls his.

"What do you care?"

I don't answer, because I'm trying to convince myself that I don't.

Fuck, what kind of witchcraft did Scarlett do on me that I'm all of a sudden...

I blink my eyes several times trying to clear the ridiculous thoughts from my head.

No, this is just a result of really good sex. I'm just dickmatized. Case closed.

"To answer your question from earlier, no, I'm not hungry. I'm actually babysitting tonight, so I'm sure that I'll end up eating Macaroni and Cheese and a pint of ice cream with Emma."

The rest of the drive is silent until he pulls off into a secluded area. It's nearing dusk, and it's getting colder by the minute so the area is pretty deserted. I don't have a chance to ask what we're doing when his face is across the console and his hand is behind my neck hauling my lips towards his. I whimper against his lips, but I let out a sigh when his thick tongue finds mine. "You bite your lip so fucking much," he tells me when he pulls back slightly. "I can't stop picturing my dick between them."

"You have a date," I whisper.

"Why do you care?"

"I don't."

"Liar."

"We hate each other. I don't care what you do, Vince."

"I don't hate you, Michaels. I'm actually quite fond of parts of you. Particularly a delicious one between your legs." His sinful words resonate throughout my whole body and a shiver runs through me.

"*I* hate you."

"Well, then hate fuck me." His lips form a crooked grin and I can feel my defenses lowering quickly.

"We said one time," I combat, but my efforts are weak.

"I'm asking for a second time." His voice is almost pleading.

"Why should I give you anything?"

"Because you're as desperate to feel my dick inside of you as I am to feel your pussy wrapped around it."

"False."

"Then why are your thighs squeezed together so hard?" His tongue runs up my neck and he nibbles gently on my earlobe. I turn my head towards his, brushing my lips against his.

"We shouldn't do this."

"I'm well aware." His lips ghost across my cheeks and down to my mouth when his phone begins to ring. I didn't mean to look, *and by that, I mean I totally meant to look*, but seeing a woman's name pop up on his screen makes my blood run cold.

"Let me get this."

"Are you fucking serious?"

"Do you want me to cancel this date or not?"

"I don't want you to do anything honestly. We aren't together. Take the call. We're good."

I don't miss the look that crosses his face before he shakes his head at me. "Hey, Darcy." His voice floods the car and then silence. I can feel his gaze on the side of my face and then he speaks again. "Yeah ummm, I'm running a little late. I got caught up with work. But um…" He pauses and I can still feel his gaze. "I'll be there."

He hangs up the phone after a few pleasantries and starts the car. "Lauren…"

"I'm good."

He sighs and I definitely don't miss the word *infuriating* escape him in a whisper.

"Auntie Lo, Auntie Lo!" Emma is running around the kitchen with her Cinderella costume on complete with her tiara and "glass slippers" when I get home. Emma looks exactly like her mother and I did when we were kids, with long chocolate brown hair and green eyes. The only difference is the dusting of freckles she has all across her nose and cheeks. "I've been waiting for you!" She runs into my arms just as I drop to the ground and scoop her up.

"Is that so? Did your mom get you hopped up on sugar just in time for them to go out?"

"I only had like six Oreos!" she says holding up two hands.

"Six huh?" I look towards the stairs, cursing my sister and brother-in-law.

"Can we play tea party?"

"Em, can we just have a movie night?" I ask as I feel the exhaustion of the past few days catching up with me.

Breaking up with Drew, getting hammered, staying out all night much of which I spent getting bent into about ten different positions, and then working all day all the while trying to make sense of my very complicated feelings for my office enemy turned…fuck frenemy?

I am tired as fuck.

"Tea *at* the movies," Emma negotiates.

"Fine, but can you give me an hour? I have to work on a story." *Aka nap.*

"One hour, Auntie Lo." She puts her tiny finger up next to her face and wiggles it and I can't help the chuckle that leaves my lips.

TINY KISSES ALL OVER MY FACE WAKE ME UP AND I OPEN an eye to see that not only is Emma in my bed, but she'd put on all my makeup, so now I'm sure my face is covered in bright red lipstick. "Really, Emma?"

She smiles. "Do I look pretty!?"

"Surprisingly, yes, good blush choice." I point at her as I manage to pull myself out of bed and walk to the adjoining bathroom. "Your mom and dad leave?"

"Yes, they were leaving when I came in to wake you up." She follows me into the bathroom, dragging her gray bear that is never far behind. "Where do you get babies?" she asks suddenly.

I look down at her and then at the mirror,

wondering how in the world I got stuck with the task of having this conversation with my very inquisitive niece. "What do you mean?"

"Well, Daddy said that they'd be back with a baby in mommy's belly. Is that where they're going tonight? To get the baby?"

I snort and roll my eyes at my brother-in-law's consistent ability to never check the room for little ears. "Did your Daddy say that to you?"

"No, they were in their room, but I heard it!" She presses her bear to her face to hide her eyes.

She knows better. "What did we tell you about eavesdropping?"

She drops the bear and looks up at me with her signature 'don't yell at me' eyes. "I don't even know what that word means!"

"Yes, you do, we talked about not listening to conversations that you're not a part of." I raise an eyebrow at her and she lowers her face.

Her bottom lip juts out in a pout. "But no one talks to me."

I kneel in front of her and begin wiping the makeup off her face. "Don't start that, I talk to you all the time. More than I talk to anyone and your parents are very attentive. You're just nosy."

"I want to be a journalist like you Auntie Lo! I gotta know all the tea!"

"Oh my God, have you been watching Bravo again?"

I stand up, leaving the makeup wipe in her hand so she can finish cleaning her face.

"No. Mommy put parental controls on, and I can't crack the code!" She shoots me a mischievous grin and I shake my head.

"Hey, I don't know what it is." I put my hands up. "Are you hungry?" I ask her as we make our way out of my bedroom and down the stairs.

"No, Mommy cooked before she left! She left some for you in the refrigerator." I sigh in relief when I see the chicken piccata. My sister is an excellent cook and despite the five pounds I've gained while living here, it's definitely one thing I'll miss when I move. I heat the chicken as Emma takes off in search of her tea set and something to watch tonight. I pull up my Instagram app and immediately watch Charley's story as usual and I smile when I see her daughter, Ana's happy face. She is the cutest and Will and Charley are adjusting to parent life well considering Will is barely sleeping. Charley says there were nights he just stares at Ana to make sure she's still breathing.

I *heart* the story before messaging her that I can't wait to see her and Ana next month. Within thirty seconds, my phone rings to life. "Oh my God, why didn't you call me?"

I groan, hearing my best friend's voice who's probably just recently heard that Drew and I broke up. "It's been…a day."

"I don't care, what the fuck? Will is pissed by the way."

"Why?"

"Because you're family! And because I'm pissed. Fucking fuckboy."

"So, you know all the details then?"

"I don't know much about her; Will says it's 'not our business,'" she says using her therapist voice that she uses when she's imitating him.

"So, he hasn't met her?" I lean against the refrigerator, hating the pitiful sound of my voice, but also wanting to know everything.

"No."

"How are you?" I ask, wanting to change the subject.

She sighs and I half expect to hear the latest Diana Montgomery drama but she squeals instead. "I'm getting married in twenty-seven days! I never thought I could be so happy. I have a baby and I love Will so much. He's actually perfect. I would be annoyed if I didn't get to benefit from said perfection." She giggles and I grab the bottle of wine from the counter and pour myself a small glass. I'm happy for Charley. She's been to hell and back in the last year and deserves this happily ever after.

I'm just hoping mine isn't far behind.

"Is it going to be weird being paired up with Drew? I can have you girls walk down the aisle separately." I can hear the concern in her voice, and instantly I'm reminded of one of the reasons I love Charley so much.

She is as selfless as they come and I know if I tell her I don't want to see Drew's face let alone walk down the aisle with him, she'd find a way to have him banned from the wedding. Charley goes hard for the people she loves, and she loves me.

"No, whatever you want, Charley. It's your day." I try my best to sound convincing, but I can hear the hurt in my voice, and I know she can hear it too.

"Shut up. I'm changing it. I'm not about to have Drew have my best girl upset."

"Can you just not give him a plus one?" I chuckle, *half* kidding.

"Done."

"Wait…I'm kidding." *Sort of.*

"I'm not. He's not bringing some ho to my wedding that will be irrelevant in two minutes. Please!"

I hear a deep voice in the background followed by Charley's voice. "Well, she is! Babe, he's not going to marry her and I don't want any awkwardness on our wedding day. It's already going to be a struggle keeping our mothers apart."

I wince hearing about their moms and their very frenemy type relationship. "Ooh, still trouble in paradise?"

"I swear Will's mom and my mom are going to drive me insane."

"Phew, your in-laws." I sigh. "You sure you're ready for this?"

"I just had his baby; I can't leave him now!"

She squeals again. "Ouch! That actually hurt, Will." She chuckles.

"Talk about leaving me again." I hear him and then a loud kiss. "Hey Lauren," he says loud and clear and I realize I must be on speakerphone.

"Hot Doc," I respond with a laugh using my nickname for him as the microwave beeps and I pull my chicken out.

"I'm sorry about my brother…" He trails off.

"You don't have to apologize, but thank you."

"You're still family to me, you know that right?"

I roll my eyes. Will is always getting sentimental; I guess it's the therapist in him. "I mean yeah, I get Ana if you two die, right?"

Charley laughs and Will sighs into the phone. "You are the lesser of two evils, I suppose."

"I take that as a compliment."

"I'm going to go check on Ana and start dinner," Will says in an attempt to give us some privacy, I'm sure. The Will I know hates being away from Charlotte for longer than a few minutes, and when they're in the same room his lips are attached to her in some way.

"Okay, I'll be down in a sec," Charley says and then I hear the sounds of another kiss. "I love you."

"I love you, and I want Ana in bed early tonight."

"Hmmm, what did you have in mind, Doctor Montgomery?" She purrs and I almost choke on my wine.

"STILL ON THE PHONE!" I yell into the phone

before I start hearing about whatever role play adventure they're embarking on tonight.

"Oops!" Charley giggles. "Listen, I'm not giving Drew a plus one, and I will do my best to play interference so that his entire family doesn't smother you. Diana is going to die when she hears. I'm still convinced she likes you more than me."

"She does like me more than you, Charley."

It's strange, but I suppose it has to do with the fact that Drew was overwhelmingly the favorite child growing up. It's kind of sad, but that changed the second Ana was born. They still aren't crazy about how Will and Charlotte started but Diana and J.R. are happy as fuck to be grandparents and, surprisingly, assumed the roles well.

"Well, fuck you," she says, and I snort into my wine before taking a sip.

"Em, did you pick a movie?" I call into the other room.

"I'm setting up the tea!!" I hear screamed in response and I'm immediately wondering what we're using for tea and more importantly, if it's all over the carpet.

"Oh, squeeze Emma for me," Charley says.

"Will do. Kiss Ana for me."

"Definitely. I'm sorry again about Drew." I hear the sadness in her voice. We'd been excited to be somewhat sisters by marriage and for our kids to be cousins. But hell, we were sisters by something stronger than anything on paper.

"Don't worry about it. He wasn't the one. Glad I learned it before he moved here."

"Well, there's a silver lining."

I walk into the living room to see that Emma has set up a fort and that thankfully she's just used water for the tea, which, of course, is all over the beige carpet.

"Lord, okay I gotta go, Charley."

"Auntie Charleeeey!" Emma calls and I put her on speakerphone so they can have a brief chat as I try to soak up the water on the floor.

A few minutes later, we're settled into the fort and I've set up Beauty and the Beast for the hundredth time.

"You ever get tired of this movie?" I ask her as she snuggles against me.

"Never! A beast turned prince, what could be better?"

I chuckle internally thinking about what this could mean for her dating life if she's already got this mentality.

A beast turned prince, huh?

I chastise myself instantly when Vince's face flashes through my mind.

6

LAUREN

We are barely through the first song in the movie before Emma is passed out against me, snoring softly. I try to move her, but she just snuggles closer to me and whimpers. I give her a look, knowing somehow, she did it on purpose so that she wouldn't have to sleep in her own bed tonight, but I let it slide because I love Beauty and the Beast too and I wouldn't mind finishing it. About an hour later, my phone begins to ring and reluctantly I pull my gaze away from Belle heading to the West Wing despite my begging her not to and frown when I see the name glaring on my screen.

INCOMING CALL
Vince

Ugh, what does he want? I let my head fall back to the couch and let out a breath, preparing my nerves for him to inevitably get on them. "What?" I answer as soon as the call connects.

"Don't answer the phone like that."

"Like what?"

"*That.* Is that any way to talk to the man that made you come four times last night?"

"I'm hanging up."

"Wait wait…Lauren, stop."

"Stop what?"

"Being…yourself."

I frown at the phone, pulling it away slightly when I note the time. "Are you drunk, Maddox?"

"No…well…yes."

"Goodbye."

"Wait! I want to talk to you?"

"People in hell want ice water, try again."

"I didn't mean to phrase that as a question."

"I don't give a fuck what you didn't mean. I'm with my niece."

"And I'm outside," he responds instantly.

"What the fuck?" I crane my head towards the window as if I would be able to see if he was telling the truth. "Why?"

"Because I want to see you, obviously."

"Weren't you on a date? With…Darcy?" I hear the jealousy in my voice and I immediately chastise myself for being so obvious.

"I left the date early. I said I wasn't feeling well."

"Because you got drunk?"

"No, the drinking came later. I got pissed that you were fucking with my head…Jesus Lauren, can I come in? It's cold as fuck out here."

"How'd you get here?"

"Uber. Can we do this chit-chat inside? Preferably over whiskey?"

I bite my bottom lip and look down at the tiny person snuggled against me.

"You can't be loud; Emma is sleeping in the living room."

"Fine, just let me in. Please."

"I'm not having sex with you while I'm babysitting," I tell him firmly, although my pussy is already arguing with me about that. I can't ignore the dull throb that's been thumping between my legs ever since his name flashed across my screen.

I could have sworn I heard him say, "We'll see about that," just as I end the call. I pick Emma up from where we were on the floor, and tuck her into the couch, leaving the pillow fort just below, in case she decides to roll around. I move towards the door, but not before taking a quick look in the mirror. I fluff my hair once, before bending over to shake some body back into it. I flip my hair back over and run my tongue over my teeth and my lips to wet them.

Not a lot of time to do much, but this will do.

I fling the door open to see Vince breathing into his

hands. He lets them drop when he sees me and then he's through the front door and pushing me inside. "Hey!" I whisper as he shuts the door behind us.

He looks me over and I follow his gaze noting my black leggings tucked into bright blue fuzzy socks and my University of Atlanta sweatshirt that has seen better days. "Even when you look like shit, you're gorgeous." He smiles and I put my hands on my hips in response.

"Again, compliment or insult?"

"Compliment," he says firmly. Now that he's inside I take a moment to look at what he'd worn on this date. Black jeans that complement his firm, muscular legs and a gray sweater that stretched across his torso almost perfectly under a black wool coat. He looks stylish in an effortless way and I find myself irritated that he looked *this* good while on a date with another woman.

He takes a step towards me and lifts my chin with his index finger to meet his gaze. "I couldn't fucking stop thinking about you." His voice is low and swirls around me, intoxicating me. I take a step back and he takes one in tandem. "You and what Scarlett said."

"I thought you didn't buy it," I interrupt.

"I didn't. I don't…"

"You're here for pussy, don't kid yourself *or* me." I roll my eyes and retreat towards the kitchen. I hear him behind me and then I feel his hand wrapping around my forearm.

"Stop being a brat, Michaels."

"Excuse me? I'm being a brat because I'm not falling to my knees at the idea that you want to fuck again?" I snort as I pull out of his grasp and move into the kitchen. I grab a bottle of water from the fridge but I feel the heat of him at my back even before I turn around. When I turn to face him, he's in my space staring down at me.

"I was thinking I'd be the one on my knees, but I'm not picky."

I chew the inside of my cheek at his innuendo, begging my hormones not to take over my voice. "No," I whisper.

"Why not?"

"Because I don't like you, and we agreed it was a one-time thing."

"I'd like to renegotiate that agreement." I don't respond and he must take that as some level of compliance because his hands find my hips and then he lifts me to set me on the countertop. "I know you hate me. You're not my favorite person either..." He swallows and makes a face, almost like he didn't like the way those words tasted. "Although, I'm warming up to you."

"I'm not interested in dating."

"Whoa, me either." He puts his hands up. "I was thinking more of a friends with benefits situation."

"We aren't friends," I correct and he huffs in response.

"Fine, enemies with benefits. Is that better?"

I narrow my eyes into slits at his proposition. "What does that entail?"

"I get to eat your pussy whenever I fucking feel like it, Michaels, what do you think?" he asks as if to say, *obviously.*

"Are you doing this with…other women?"

"I left a very sure thing tonight because I couldn't stop thinking about the way your nipples pucker when I blow on them. No, Michaels, I'm not."

My nipples tighten on their own, like my body knew that Vince had spoken about them. "I'm not looking for…"

He steps closer, running his tongue along my bottom lip. "You don't have to do all of that. I don't want that."

"So just…sex?"

"Yeah. I want to use this pretty little body for my pleasure." He moves his hand between my legs to stroke me through my leggings.

I grab his hand, squeezing it so that he'll stop and I can try to focus. "What's so special about me, anyway?"

He crosses his arms and leans against the counter before giving me a wicked smirk. "I'm not sure. I was hoping your mouth around my cock again would give me clarity."

"This is going to get messy, you know that, right?"

His hands find my face and for a moment, I think I

see something in his eyes behind the haze of liquor. "I know you like to be in control of every situation. I know you like to weigh the pros and cons and not make any hasty decisions based on emotions, but for once can you just go with the flow?"

"One of us is going to get hurt. You know that's how this works right? Haven't you seen any romance movie ever?"

He takes a step back. "This has nothing to do with romance. Do you want to fuck me again?" I look away from his gaze and let out a sigh before nodding my head. "Words please, Lauren."

"Yes."

"And I sure as fuck want to do the same, like right the fuck now."

"No."

"Then at least let me taste you." He leans forward again, grabbing my bottom lip between his teeth and pulling before letting go. "Let me fuck you with my tongue. I want to run my lips over that sinfully sweet cunt of yours. Lap up everything your body has to offer the second you orgasm. Do you know I can actually feel your clit pulse when you come? It's the sexiest fucking thing I've ever experienced in bed."

My mouth drops open at his words and before I can give it a second thought my leggings and panties have hit the floor and he's on his knees in front of me. His hands slide up my legs to my thighs and he grips me hard before he attacks my folds with an urgency I've never experienced. Maybe because I'm sober now, I can feel everything. The way he explores my pussy, the way he sucks and licks and bites the sensitive flesh between my legs.

"Holy shit, Vince," I cry out, before slapping a hand over my mouth. He slides his tongue through my entrance fucking me for a few seconds before drawing his attention to my clit. My hands move into his hair, baring my nails and scratching slightly causing his hands to grip me harder.

God, if you're up there, please just make sure Emma stays asleep.

I look down at the man feasting between my thighs and let out a quiet moan.

God is not listening right now.

His eyes meet mine and I see the smile in them as he spreads my sex with his fingers. "How close are you, beautiful?" His hands find their way underneath me, cupping my bottom as he pulls me harder against his mouth.

"Close," I whisper, as I'm trying my best not to scream as the beginning of a spectacular orgasm begins to move through me. I can't look away as our eyes lock during this heated moment.

Fuck, why does he look at me like that? It's like he can see everything.

I try to look away when he bites gently on my clit. Not hard, but it's enough to turn my attention back to him. "Eyes on me," he growls as he slides two fingers into my wet pussy. I shatter against his mouth, and I grip the back of his head, pushing him harder against me as the aftershocks of the most delicious orgasm I've ever had start rolling through me.

"Holy fuck!" I say a little bit louder than I intended and instantly take my lip between my teeth to quiet my cries. He stands in front of me and presses his lips to mine to muffle the screams bubbling in my throat. His hands weave through my hair and I close my eyes, relishing in this kiss. He pulls away from my lips, peppering kisses along my jawline and down my neck. His tongue darts out and licks at my pulse point before dragging upwards behind my ear.

"Can I stay?"

"Vince." I'm trying my best to tell him no, but his name on my lips is a weak plea at best. A plea not to push too hard because I will give in.

I don't answer his question, I just push him away and hop off the counter to pull my pants and underwear back on and make my way out of the kitchen to check on Emma. To my surprise, she's still sprawled out on the couch fast asleep.

I hear a chuckle behind me. "She's cute. She looks just like you."

"Her mom and I are twins," I tell him to better explain why Emma looks so much like a younger version of me.

"Oh, be still my heart," he says putting a hand over it and I roll my eyes.

"My sister is happily married; don't get any pervy ideas."

"Just let me picture it, who am I hurting?"

"You're annoying me," I tell him as I pick Emma up and rub her back gently in case, I accidentally wake her up.

"You want me to carry her?" Vince asks and I shake my head.

"No, you stay here, I'm just going to lay her down." I kiss her forehead as I make my way upstairs and I'm able to get her into bed without waking her, thankfully. I rush into my bathroom to quickly brush my teeth, swipe a few coats of mascara on my lashes and a bit of lip balm. I change my bra and my panties, apply some deodorant and put on a t-shirt that showcases my breasts way more than a ratty sweatshirt.

When I move back downstairs, I see Vince is staring at pictures on the mantle. "Hey."

He turns around and smiles. "You didn't have to change, I thought you looked hot. Like a young co-ed."

"Of course, you did." I roll my eyes at the thought that men loved when a woman looks like borderline jailbait.

He sits on the couch and I sit next to him when he pulls me into his lap. "You don't really hate me, do you?"

"I don't hate you, but you're pretty infuriating," I tell him.

"You're no walk in the park either, sunshine."

"So…frenemies with benefits?" I let the words come out slowly, allowing myself to mull over each word. "We can't fuck at the office."

He snorts as a mischievous grin finds his face. "Yeah, we'll see."

7

LAUREN

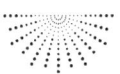

"Auntie Lo."

I open one eye to find my niece standing in front of me, her head cocked to one side so she can stare at me. Her hair is perfectly brushed and pulled into a high ponytail and I can't help the smile pulling at my lips at her ability to groom herself.

"What time is it?" My voice is still thick with sleep, so I clear my throat as she picks up my phone from the nightstand.

"Six three six." She points at each number.

I groan at the ungodly hour at which she's woken me up. "Go back to bed, munchkin."

She furrows her brow and I notice her peeking over my shoulder. "Auntie Lo," she whispers before she points behind me, "there's a boy in your bed." I don't mistake the chuckle behind me alerting me that said boy is awake. "Who is that?"

"Umm," *Fuck.* "a friend," I tell her.

"Did you guys have a sleepover?" Her wide eyes and large smile showcase her innocence.

"Something like that."

"No fun," she pouts. "I fell asleep. What did you guys do?"

Another chuckle fills the air and I jam my heel into his shin. He hisses and circles an arm around my middle which thankfully is covered by my blanket.

I pull away from his grasp and sit up, grateful that I'd had the foresight to put on pants after Vincent had proceeded to make me come with his mouth *twice.*

"Emma, go back to bed," I tell her as I get up and guide her towards the open door and gently push her through it.

"Wait! Can I meet him?" She looks up at me, her green eyes large and questioning before she lets her bottom lip jut out in that way that always makes me give in to whatever she wants.

"He's sleeping."

"Is not, look!" She points behind me, and reluctantly I turn around to see him sitting up in bed with a smile playing on his lips. He waves and she runs past me and stands next to his side of the bed.

"Hi, Emma, I've heard a lot about you." He smiles that crooked smile and my niece beams under his charm just like every other female in the world.

"Really!? Who are you? Auntie Lo never has boys over for sleepovers." She looks at me, and I narrow my gaze at her. She's five and doesn't quite understand that my look means to 'stop talking,' so she shrugs and turns back to Vince.

His eyes flit to mine in response to her statement and he quirks his brow in question. "Is that so?"

"Nope, you wanna stay for breakfast?" She bounces on the balls of her feet like she does when she's excited.

"No no no angel, he's busy!" I tell her quickly and her eyes dart to his.

"Too busy for pancakes? My mommy makes the best." She points at her chest accompanied by a smile of pride.

He looks at me and I shake my head. There is no way I'm about to explain to my family why Vincent Maddox, *who my sister is very familiar with* has stayed the night.

"Thank you so much for inviting me, but...I do have to work. Maybe some other time?"

She frowns, probably at being told no which is not a concept that she's familiar with before looking up at me. "Do you work with Auntie Lo?"

"I sure do."

"Oh! You're a writer too?"

And here comes the Emma inquisition.

"I am." He nods and I'll admit watching him entertain my niece makes me warm in places I don't want to admit.

"That's so cool. I want to be a writer!"

"Okay, Em..." I grab her hand and pull her gently. "Time to go."

"Okay wait wait wait, I have one more question!" She gives me a pleading look as she looks up at me.

"Okay, make it quick."

"Are you the guy Auntie Lo says is hotter than sin?" She looks up at me. "Maybe you should get him some ice water?"

"HOTTER THAN SIN, HUH?" VINCE SAYS AS SOON AS I SHUT the door behind us. I had managed to sneak him out no more than five minutes after I'd ushered my niece out the door, and now we are outside in the freezing cold as we wait for his Uber.

I bite my bottom lip and narrow my eyes at him. "Fuck. Off."

He takes a step towards me and presses me against the house, the cool bricks freezing my back.

"I tried to fuck you this morning…and last night, if I recall correctly, and with more than just my tongue." His lips brush against mine and down my jawline to my neck. He pushes my coat open and presses his hand against my mound, cupping me over the thin pants covering my naked sex.

"Vince." My eyes flutter closed as he puts pressure on my clit, stroking me gently. The heat from my pussy mixed with the cold wind whipping against my legs creates a dizzy feeling throughout my whole body and I'm resisting the urge to push him to the ground and rub myself against his cock until I come. I swallow hard and shake my head. "Your…Uber." I point behind him as I notice the black Nissan pull to a stop in front of the house.

"I'll see you Monday." He grips my jaw, grabs my bottom lip between his teeth, and tugs hard. "Wear those sexy thigh highs of yours. I want to pull those off with my teeth while your cunt drips all over my desk."

AGAINST MY BETTER JUDGMENT, I DO WEAR THOSE THIGH highs on Monday, along with a pair of black panties that leave nothing to the imagination. A sexy idea that I had not thought through because it isn't doing much to mask the wetness between my legs that I'm dying for Vincent to lick up with that sinful mouth of his.

My boss, however, has other plans.

"This is great, you guys," he says as he looks over the piece on Scarlett Stone. We'd done most of it virtually, sharing a Google Doc file, between intermittent sexting over the weekend, and had finished it up this morning over coffee and eye fucking.

I'm so wound up and ready to come. Now.

"Great," I chirp, fully prepared to get up and leave when Jack looks at me curiously. "Two marriages?" We'd included bits and pieces of my reading and Vince thought it was imperative to include that.

I roll my eyes and try to avoid eye contact with the

man sitting next to me. "Vince's idea. Apparently, 'it explains a lot.'"

"It's cheeky and perfect for Twitter. Good work." He sets the paper down. "Maybe I should have you guys work on things more often. Both of your voices come through loud and clear, kind of like a debate. It's different. I like it." He leans back in his chair and eyes us both over his lenses. "Would you be open to doing more together?"

I blink several times as if I'm trying to convince my brain that it isn't an innuendo or a metaphor for doing *it* together.

"Vince?" I risk a look, and it's as if my body is set ablaze by the look he gives back. It's hungry and a bit dangerous as he rakes his gaze from my feet to my eyes. I turn away instantly, to avoid being openly eye fucked in front of our boss.

He clears his throat and turns back to Jack. "Lauren and I have a new *understanding* of each other. I think we'll work together just fine again."

"Mmmmhmm. I'll bet. Just keep it out of the office," Jack says with a snort and a flick of his wrist, dismissing us.

My cheeks burn with embarrassment under the insinuation that he knows just what our newfound 'understanding' is, and I'm gearing up for the verbal ass-kicking I'm going to give Vince the second we step out of this office.

"Seriously?" I ask as soon as the door shuts. "Is this a

joke to you?"

"Come on, Lauren. Jack is cool." He laughs as he turns towards his office. He stops after a few steps, probably when he realizes I'm not following him and he turns back around. "You're not really mad, right?"

"Kinda!"

"Who the fuck cares what we do? I'm not your boss, it's not like you have to worry about people thinking you're sleeping your way to the top. Who gives a shit?"

"I do, and what happened to not wanting anyone in the office to know?" It was only a few days ago that we agreed that this would stay between us, and now he's telling our freaking boss? *Fuck that.*

He shrugs and leans against the wall. "You act like I announced it at the morning meeting. What's the big deal? It's not like I flat out told him, anyway."

"Because I am a lady, thank you very much, and I don't need anyone in my business."

"Okay, I'm fairly certain a 'lady' doesn't use the word 'cunt' or 'fuck' in everyday conversation or fuck their coworkers in a bar bathroom." He points at me. "And no one is in our fucking business, Lauren."

I ignore the fact that he used the word *our* and focus on the first part. "Are you slut shaming me now?"

He runs a hand through his hair and I can sense the exasperation coming off of him in waves. *Good. Now we're on the same page.* "No, oh my God, Lauren. You're doing it again."

"Doing what?"

"Being yourself. Stop. I like you better when you're relaxed," he says with a groan as he turns around and moves back towards his office. "Which seems to only happen when my dick is inside of you," he calls over his shoulder.

"Do not walk away from me." I stomp after him and follow him into his office, shutting the door behind us.

"Lock the door behind you." He gives me a cocky smile as he leans against his desk. He rolls his sleeves up and crosses his arms in front of him.

"We are not doing anything."

He huffs and rolls his eyes. "Lauren, I refuse to jack off tonight, get your ass over here." He settles into his chair behind his desk and looks up at me with those piercing blue eyes.

"No."

Why!?

"Fuck," he groans and puts his hands over his eyes. "I'm sorry Jack is a fucking journalist and read between the lines. And no, I was not slut shaming you. I've fucked actual sluts, and you are definitely not one. Happy?"

Does he know anything about women?

I ignore his comment about fucking other women because the last thing I needed is to come off jealous when Vince and I are not *anything*. This is about him telling our boss that we had sex.

Well, insinuating it.

Focus on that.

"There were no lines to read between, the way you were looking at me said it all!" I exclaim.

He gets up and crosses the room, his long legs eating at the space between us until I'm up against his door. His arms dart out, effectively boxing me in before letting one hand slide down the door to the doorknob to lock it. "I've been looking at you the same way for the past six months...maybe this is the first time *you've* noticed, but I can assure you it's not the first time Jack has." He runs a finger from my cheek down my side, leaving my skin tingling in its wake. I feel myself melting under his gaze. "You're infuriating." *Way to kill the moment, asshole.*

"I am not," I snap.

He chuckles at my petulant tone. "I have a conference call in twenty minutes, can I eat your pussy before then or what?"

I take a step towards his desk, fully prepared to sit on top of it and let him do just that despite my slight annoyance when my phone begins to ring. I look down and my eyes widen in shock with the name flashing across my screen.

Why is Drew calling?

Before I have a chance to tell myself that I should definitely let the phone call from my ex-boyfriend roll to voicemail and let Vince put his mouth on my cunt, I'm pressing the phone to my ear. "Hi."

8

LAUREN

"**D**id you tell Charley to take away my plus one to my own fucking brother's wedding? The wedding, *my* parents are paying for?" My ex's aggressive voice rings through the phone making me feel like someone has just knocked the wind out of me. I never knew Drew Montgomery to raise his voice and definitely not at me. But hearing the venom shooting through the phone is enough to make me want to end this call.

Why did I answer this phone call?

Why did I think anything good would come from this?

Did I think he was calling to get me back?

"First of all, Will is paying for most of it, as you know, so you can fuck off about Daddy's money. Secondly, no, I did not. Maybe Charley cares about my feelings just a bit more than your new girlfriend who probably won't be around till the end of the month."

He chuckles and I feel a flash of anger shooting through me at his response. "Bitterness doesn't suit you, Lauren."

I snort. "You're being an asshole, and I don't have time for it. I'm at work."

"This is fucking ridiculous. This wedding isn't about you."

"It's about you and your new flavor of the month? I'm sorry I could have sworn it was about my best friend and your brother, who pretty much hated you until a year ago." The line goes silent. I know it was a low blow, and I'll admit I feel a bit guilty, especially when I see the look Vince is giving me. He makes a gesture that I needed to hang up the phone and when I don't respond he moves towards me.

After a few moments, Drew speaks again. "Alright then, I guess I'll see you at the wedding, Lauren."

The line goes dead before I can respond and I slide it down my face trying to blink away the tears building in my eyes at this awkward confrontation with my ex whom I'll have to face in less than three weeks.

"Did you really have to answer that?" Vince asks as he gently pulls my phone from my hand like a parent removes something they perceive to be dangerous from a child.

"I…" I watch as he sets my phone on his desk, out of my reach.

"Thought he was calling to get you back? The guy's a dick, Lauren."

I frown. "You don't even know what he said."

"I have a guess based on what you said *and* you called him an asshole."

"He is," I murmur.

"Leaving you for some other chick and telling you via text? Yeah, I'll agree with that." He sits on the small love seat in the corner of his office and pulls me into his lap. "I've never seen someone rattle you. This is the second time I've seen him get under your skin."

"He was my boyfriend, Vince. For almost a year. Of course, he knows how to rattle me."

"Fair. But you're better than that. Better than him." His lips brush against my shoulder.

"Am I? I did plant the seed with Charley...I didn't want to see him making out with his new girlfriend. It was a moment of weakness and Charley ran with it."

He chuckles. "Sounds like your girl's got your back."

"She's the best." I smile as I recall how deep my friendship with Charley goes. She loves me through poor fashion choices and my terrible idea to get bangs. We shared an address for more than three years in college and managed to not kill each other.

She was there when my father got sick. When he got better...and then when he got sick again but *didn't* get better. She held my hand at the funeral and let me cry for two straight days while she all but forced food down my throat. Charley went above and beyond for me, always.

"You know what you need?" Vince asks, breaking my trip down memory lane.

"An orgasm?"

"Well, yes, but we don't have time for that now since you decided to have a battle of wits with your ex, so no, something better."

"What's that?" I ask as I wonder what could possibly be better than an orgasm right now.

"Well, *you've* got a plus one, don't you?"

"Well...I guess? I don't really have one since Drew is in the wedding, but I'm sure I could ask Charley."

"You need a date to this wedding." He taps my nose and I scrunch it in response.

I look at him curiously. "Why?"

"You want to hurt your ex? Jealousy is the way to do it. Show up with another guy and it will drive Drew insane. Especially because you got his new girl uninvited. It's the perfect karma."

"Doesn't that make me a little...vindictive?"

"And calling out his family drama doesn't?"

"I was not being vindictive! A little petty, yes. But it's true. Besides, who am I going to find on short notice? It's not like I've been dating. Drew and I broke up three days ago."

"No...not dating." He leans back and it causes me to fall with him, further into his lap. He tugs on the ends of my hair and sweeps it over my shoulder. "But you are sleeping with someone who may be willing to help you stick it to him."

"You? You want to come to Atlanta? Like as my date?"

"I mean…only to not make a liar out of Scarlett Stone."

Three Weeks Later

I let out a deep sigh as I settle into the middle seat on the six a.m. flight that Vince told me was the best deal, and also "gives my dick ample time with your pussy before you have to run off to do wedding shit." He's lucky he's been supplying me with coffee ever since we woke up or I'd actually be as evil as Vince thinks I am.

"I am so tired."

"Well, no one told you to keep riding my dick until two." A snicker comes from the other side of me and I resist the urge to glare at the way-to-perky-for-six-a.m. blonde who fixed her gaze on Vince just a little too long as he lifted my bag into the overhead bin.

He takes a sip of his coffee innocently when I shoot him a dirty look. "Can you be any louder? I don't think the pilot heard you."

"Actually…" he says, his voice loud enough to be heard by at least five rows ahead. I slap my hand over his mouth and I can see he's smiling at me behind his eyes.

"God, are you always this annoying in the morning?" I ask as I lower my hand from his mouth, taking my time to run my fingers through the facial hair. His beard has grown out a little more than usual, and while he told me he would trim it to its usual length for the wedding, I can't stop touching it.

"Usually, but maybe you don't notice since you spend most of our mornings together sitting on my face. You're much more accepting after my tongue does that thing you like," he whispers in my ear and I shiver at his sinful words.

The sounds of people still moving down the aisle towards open seating as well as the white noise of indistinct chatter are all around me, but all I can seem to focus on is the man staring at me with blue eyes that for once seem to be filled with something *different.*

I rub my nose against his and let out a sigh when his lips brush against mine. His teeth grab my bottom lip and tug gently, causing me to let out a quiet whimper.

What is happening?

My eyes flutter closed. "You didn't this morning…"

Hands find my cheeks and he presses his lips harder against mine. "I'll make it up to you the second we're within sight range of a bed," he pauses and then shoots me his signature grin, "or we're completely alone, whichever comes first."

I pull back slowly as they lower the lights to prepare for takeoff. "Deal." I smile and he nods before holding his hand out, palm facing upwards.

I look at his hand, before looking up at him curiously. "We do the hand holding thing now?"

Sure, we're having sex, a lot of sex. We've shared a few meals together between the sex and maybe we do talk a lot when we aren't doing either, but we aren't together. We aren't dating, and holding hands just seems so...intimate? Okay, maybe intimate is the wrong word seeing as how you can't get more intimate then putting your tongue in someone's ass but that is sex. This is...

He rolls his eyes at me and sighs before lowering it slowly. "You don't like flying. Neither does my younger sister, so I hold her hand when we takeoff. Wasn't asking for your hand in marriage, Michaels." I frown, hearing him use my last name, something he hasn't done much recently. He'd taken to calling me Lauren or Lo and, in this moment, I realize how much I prefer that. He shifts his gaze out the window just as we begin to back away slowly from the gate.

"Hey," I whisper, and he looks back at me, one eyebrow quirked in question and I lift the armrest between us. "How did you know I don't like flying?"

"I heard you mention it in passing. I don't really remember when; one of the times you were flying home to Atlanta."

The idea that Vince had stored away that random piece of knowledge sparks something inside of me. Something I haven't felt. Maybe ever. I don't respond to his comment, I just press my head to his shoulder and take a deep breath, in hopes of calming my fears and also to breathe in his scent. I barely have time to unpack the thought that the feeling of Vince's arms around me and his scent burrowing into my senses calms me before I'm asleep.

9

LAUREN

The hotel where all of the guests are staying is nothing short of spectacular. I take in my surroundings of the infamous Four Seasons Hotel before I let my eyes fall on Vince who seems to have caught the attention of a few women passing by as he checks us into the hotel. I watch as one's appreciative glances move up and down his lean body and suddenly a feeling of territoriality spikes in my veins. I move towards the front desk and before I can think, my hand is sliding in his back pocket as I look up at him. "Everything good?" I blink a few times at the concierge, a woman with strawberry blonde hair who may have been struggling to focus under Vince's charm as well.

"Umm yes, sorry." She looks down and I note the blush painting her cheeks. "You're in room 700. Most of the bridal party is on that floor as well." Vince's hand slides around me and his fingertips move gently down my side, gliding over my ribcage and causing my heart to flutter slightly.

I try not to focus on his hand placement or the fact that he's moved even closer to me and his body heat is radiating off of him. "Thank you. Has Charlotte Pierce checked in yet?"

"No, but I can let her know you're here as soon as she arrives, if you'd like? You're the maid of honor, correct?" she asks just as Vince drapes an arm around my shoulder.

"Yes? How do you know that?" My hand that's still in his back pocket, grips his butt hard, in attempts to get him to stop teasing me but he just chuckles and presses his lips to my temple.

"You're going to pay for that," he whispers in my ear.

"We have a list of the bridal party given to us by the wedding planner," she answers as she shifts her gaze between us.

"Okay, wow, great. You guys are efficient. Yes, let her know I'm here. I'll be in my room." I give her a smile and pull Vince out of the lobby and away from watching eyes before he pins me to the floor and fucks the life out of me.

God knows I'd let him.

"YOU WERE AWFULLY HANDSY DOWN THERE." I RAISE MY eyebrow at him as he sets our suitcases in the room.

The suite is gorgeous. An all-white room, complete with a king bed so inviting I want to take my clothes off this second and roll around in it…with Vince. I pull my jacket off and step onto the balcony that overlooks a terrace and a gazebo filled with flowers that I'm sure Charlotte has already spotted for pictures.

"Says the woman who made a point to grab my ass." He makes his way over to me slowly uncorking the champagne that is part of the welcome basket in our room. It also includes Tylenol, water, gum, Chapstick, and various other wedding party necessities. He pops the cork and pours the bubbly liquid into two champagne flutes before handing one to me. "We're trying to make your ex jealous, aren't we?" he asks. "I gotta up my game a little."

I take a sip and give him a pointed look. "That's the *only* reason for your PDA?"

"What else would it be?" he asks as he downs his drink and heads back into the room. I follow behind him because I remember a certain promise and I'm planning to collect. "Hey," I call after him. He turns around in time to see me pulling my top over my head and sliding my leggings down my legs. "I do recall a promise of you doing that thing with your tongue."

I note something in his eyes, like he wants to say something, but it's gone in a flash and then he's on the move towards me. "Get on the bed," he commands and I don't waste a second before I'm on the move. I yank my hair from the confines of my ponytail, letting the messy waves from this morning's shower fall around me. I reach around me to unclasp my bra, letting my breasts spring free, my nipples already two hard points, heavy and aching for his touch. My sex tingles in anticipation of what's to come and I'm grateful I don't have to wait long before he's kneeling on the bed over me. "I want you to do that thing I like first."

"What's that?"

"Choke on my cock."

"That wasn't the deal." I lean back on my elbows and stare up at him. Despite my pushback, I wet my lips in preparation as he tows off his shoes and lowers his pants to the ground.

He leans down so that his lips barely touch mine. "Then why has your breathing changed? Why are you struggling to swallow past that lump in your throat? Why are you pressing your legs so tight together? Is it because you know the second I push my dick through those plump lips of yours, that space between your legs gets slicker? Because sucking my cock isn't just foreplay for me…but for you?" I let out a breath when he leans back out of my space.

"I want…I want to come first."

"Well, that's not your call, Michaels." He grips my chin hard. "Open your mouth." I comply with his order as my eyes flutter shut. I wasn't expecting him to shove his cock in my mouth, especially with this awkward angle we're in, but I wasn't expecting his tongue either. He feeds me his tongue, greedily, sloppily, letting it roam the inside of my mouth. He pushes me down into the comforter and I sink into the plushness as his body melds to mine. I wrap my legs around him, crossing my ankles behind him and pushing his cock harder against my pussy as he grinds against me. He pulls back, his lips wet with our spit and stares down at me. "You're so beautiful, Lo," he whispers before he presses his lips to mine gently. I feel his hand between us sliding my panties to the side and then he's rubbing my clit, hard at first and then in gentle circles. His fingers glide easily, because if I'm being honest, I've been wet since he made that scene in front of the woman in the lobby.

Things are changing between Vince and me. I can see it in his eyes and feel it in his touch. I'm not sure what these changes mean, only that the last of our hate for each other seems to be floating away with every swipe over my clit. "Vince, I don't...I don't want to come like this."

"Mmm. Not all over my fingers?" he whispers in my ear and I shake my head, the words failing me as my eyes float back.

"No…"

"But why? You love it. You love humping my hand, riding my fingers like it's my cock."

"But it's not…I need…" I grip his shirt, trying to tether myself from getting swept away in this storm brewing beneath my skin. "Please fuck me," I beg. "Please!"

"But you're doing so well. God, you should see how

you look beneath me. You're so fucking perfect right now." He kisses my forehead, trailing his lips down my face before reaching my lips and dragging his tongue along the seam. "Come for me, Lauren."

"But…"

"Don't make me tell you again," he growls in my ear and just as I feel myself at the edge, a jarring noise brings me back.

"LAUREN LAUREN LAUREN!!!" I hear squealed through the door and my eyes fly open at my best friend's voice. The knocking continues and I hear her voice she uses for Ana. "You want to see Auntie Lo!? Yes, you do!"

"Fuck." I half cry, half moan as Vince's fingers are still inside me. He pulls them out slowly and runs his tongue over his fingers lasciviously. I resist the urge to ignore my best friend's knocks and climb on top of him.

He looks at the door and back at me as he slides his pants back over his legs. "Lauren, are you in there?!" I hear again and I roll my eyes.

"One second!" I yell as I pull my clothes on as well. I take a step towards the door before turning back around and grabbing Vince's face and pull his lips to mine. "Five minutes," I whisper against his lips. "I still want your cock." I wink.

Tears flood the bright blue eyes of my best friend the second I open the door and I take a second to look her over. She looks gorgeous, glowing in that special way that all brides do. She'd been on an intense diet that both Will and I had tried to talk her out of as well as two-a-day workouts at the gym. But I'll admit, it has paid off because she looks fucking amazing. Her skin is glowing and her hair never looked healthier. But on top of all that, she looks happier than I've ever seen her.

Being in love can do that.

"Oh my God!" She's in my arms in an instant, squeezing me despite the infant in her arms. Ana giggles reminding us she's there and I pull her from her mother's arms instantly. "My angel!" I press kisses to her tiny face and watch as she smiles. "The happiest baby on Earth."

Charley follows me further into the room and I brace myself for the interrogation that's to come when Charley puts it together just who my plus one is.

"So, wait, where's your…" She stops when she spots Vince on the bed.

"Oh… hi?" Her curious eyes dart from me to Vince and the slightly disheveled sheets before turning back to me with a curious look.

"I'm Charlotte." She gives him a polite smile before holding her hand out.

"Vince Maddox." He nods before giving her his winning grin and shaking her hand.

"I know who you are." A smirk finds her lips and she gives me a look that says *we are so talking about this later.* "Well, it seems like you two were busy before we barged in." She looks at me and plucks her daughter from my arms. "I'll leave you be for an hour and then I need you."

"Deal."

"Drew is going to die." She chuckles before turning to Vince. "And so is my future mother-in-law... I'm so happy you're here." She winks and then she's gone leaving the scent of her Burberry perfume in her wake.

Returning to the bed is long forgotten after Charlotte leaves. Both of us want to wash the travels off of us which is how we end up in the shower that is bigger than Vince's office. His hands make their way into my hair, rubbing the minty smelling shampoo in my tresses and I moan when I feel his nails against my scalp. "You make the sexiest noises." His hands drop from my hair and find my nipples, tweaking them between his fingers.

"Vince, fuck."

"Is that what you want," he whispers against my temples. "For me to fuck you...now?"

I nod, my voice temporarily lost as the assault on my breasts takes over. I turn around to rinse the suds out of my hair and just as my eyes close, I feel lips at my sex. "Ah!" I brace myself against the wall just as his hands move up my legs to grip my ass. He stands after a few seconds and pushes me back gently so I can sit on the marble bench in the corner of the shower. He spreads my legs and presses his mouth to my sex, licking away the water and the arousal between my legs. He looks up at me, his eyes dark and hungry before sucking my slippery clit into his mouth and I lose it. With one hand at the back of his head and one behind me to keep myself steady, I ride out one of the most intense orgasms of my life just as he slips two fingers inside me to push me even further. "FUCK."

I've never felt like this, I've never come like this, and somewhere in my brain is working overtime to figure out why. He licks me past my orgasm to the point that I'm trembling against him as he tongues my over sensitized clit. He pulls back finally and I press a hand to my chest to calm my racing heart. "Holy shit." I bite my bottom lip as I let my greedy eyes roam all over his naked wet body. My eyes pass over his strong muscular arms, his broad tanned chest, and the abs that sit just beneath before that stunning V that leads to his cock. He leans back and I trace my gaze over his dick, watching as it gets harder with each passing second and I long to run my tongue along the veiny purple lines. I move off the bench and between his legs to wrap my hand around him.

He swats my hand away and grabs my hips pulling me on top of him. He lets me hover above him for an instant, his eyes asking me the question. I swallow hard, as the vulnerability of this moment takes me over. We haven't had sex without protection, but in this moment, I want nothing more than skin to skin contact. I nod in response and he lowers me slowly onto his dick, bucking up into me just as I sheath myself completely.

"Fuck, Lauren. Your pussy…it's incredible."

I wrap my arms around his neck and press my lips to the space behind his ear, a move I know drives him crazy as I start to ride him. "It's so deep." I can't tell if the wetness from my cheeks is from the shower or if the tears that had welled in my eyes have trickled down but I'm suddenly overwhelmed with emotions.

Maybe it's because my best friend is getting remarried. Maybe it's anxiety over facing Drew. Or maybe, and somewhere deep I believe it to be the actual reason, I am finding myself falling for Vince Maddox. The cocky asshole with a God complex has made me fall for him. That despite our arguments and back and forth and battles of wits, he's found his way into my mind and my heart.

How did this happen?

"Looks like you're finally about where I am." His hands find my cheeks and my eyes widen at what seems to be his ability to read my mind.

"What do you mean?" I stop moving, his dick still buried inside me bare and pulsing.

"You drive me crazy, Lauren Michaels." His eyes are sincere and his long lashes make them seem even brighter in the shower. "But I'm fucking crazy about you."

10

VINCE

SIX MONTHS PRIOR

"**T**ell me you've seen the new girl." Dax from sales drops into the chair in my office and takes a sip of his coffee. "Smoke. Fucking. Show." He points at me and I turn my gaze away from the article I've been working on. I lift one eyebrow at him and lean back in my chair prepared to hear all about Dax's newest obsession. That was his thing, fucking the newest girls and then proceeding to hide from them for the rest of his life when things inevitably went south. I tried to tell him to stop shitting where he eats but he thinks with the head of his dick and not the one a few feet higher.

"I swear I think I'm in love."

"What happened to Rachel?"

"Eh, she was a boring lay. Man focus, I don't know how you haven't seen her, she's in your department." I frown, wondering how there's a new woman on my floor that I'm not familiar with. I knew a new guy was coming in from Atlanta…*Michael something?*

"Are you sure?"

"Dude, I just passed her, she's in this sexy little pencil skirt looking like a fucking pin-up girl. Pencil skirt, pantyhose, white blouse. If she were wearing glasses, I'd probably propose marriage on sight."

I roll my eyes. "Okay calm down, what's her name?"

"How the fuck should I know? She's gorgeous though. Looks like she's mixed with something. Maybe black and white? Or something European?"

"Not your usual type." I cock my head to the side. Dax typically went for the three B's— blonde hair, blue eyes, and batshit crazy. Well, four, because he's a breast man too, and anything below a B cup wouldn't even turn his head.

"For her, I'd say fuck my type." He shrugs and runs a hand through his blonde hair.

"Well, I'll see what I can find out," I tell him before turning back to my computer.

IT'S NOT UNTIL LATER THAT DAY, WHEN I'M GETTING BACK from an interview in the field for my next story, that I spot a woman getting on the elevator that seemed to fit Dax's description. She's in front of me, so I take a brief moment to shamelessly rake my gaze over a lean pair of legs and a slim body. Chestnut waves fall around her shoulders and I watch as she slides all of it to one side, exposing a smooth flawless neck that I want to run my tongue down.

Fuck. Dax wasn't kidding. She's fine as hell.

I follow her into the elevator and she doesn't even look up from her notes. Her eyebrows are furrowed in concentration and her lip finds her way between her teeth. She scoffs and drops the papers down to her side and lets out a breath. "Fucking amateurs."

I chuckle and genuinely wonder if she hasn't noticed me because her eyes quickly snap to mine.

"You alright," I ask her.

"Just lazy journalism." She points at the papers in her hand.

"Isn't that the worst," I offer and her lips quirk up in a smile. I see the faint signs of dimples that have always been my fucking weakness and I resist the urge to run my thumb down her cheek to feel the tiny indent.

"I'm Vince."

"I'm new," she quips and I can see the playfulness in her eyes.

"I gathered. I'd certainly remember you." I hadn't intended for that to come out so sleazy and I inwardly cringe at my own words.

Get it together, Maddox.

"Hmmm," she says just as the elevator sings and she slides out onto my floor.

I follow her, my mind already memorizing her scent and the way her hips sway with each step.

"What's your name, anyway?"

"You'll find out soon enough, Maddox." She giggles before slipping into my boss's office and promptly shutting the door in my face.

The hell?

I hadn't expected her to fall at my feet at my half assed attempt at flirting but I didn't expect to be blown off either.

IT'S IN THE LATE AFTERNOON STAFF MEETING WHEN MY boss introduces a *Lauren Michaels* to the team and I almost spit out my coffee.

"Wait…Michael is a woman?" I blurt out. *That woman?* Ten sets of eyes fall on me in response to my word vomit and I clear my throat in preparation of removing my foot from my mouth at my potentially chauvinistic comment. I watch as beautiful green eyes I'm seeing for the second time today widen slightly and then narrow in confusion.

"*Michaels*," she corrects. "My first name is Lauren. Problem?" she snaps and I can see the fire in her eyes directed only at me.

"No…I just didn't know." I shrug, shooting her a cocky grin.

The rest of the meeting is uneventful, though I caught her staring at me every once in a while. *Glaring is more like it.*

By the end of the meeting, I'm convinced that I'm not Lauren Michaels' favorite person.

Whether or not she's interested in me is a different story.

The following day

"Laura," I call after her as I spy her walking down the hall. She's wearing pants today, ones that frame her hips and complement her ass in a way that makes me wonder if they're custom made. I fall into step with her but she stops abruptly and stares at me.

"You know it's Lauren."

"Well, it's not like you introduced yourself." I lean against the wall and cross my arms.

"Jack introduced me to the entire team." She huffs and I smile in response to her feistiness. She's wearing a burgundy lipstick that accentuates her full lips especially when she purses them at me and making me wonder what it would be like to sink my teeth into them.

"Listen, if you're going on a coffee run, can you let me know?"

"Excuse me?" Rage flashes in her eyes and I smile inwardly at the ability to push her buttons.

"I like it black," I tell her before I turn around and start down the hallway.

"Are you serious?!" she calls after me, but I ignore her as I head back into my office.

A WEEK GOES BY AND OUR BANTER ONLY INTENSIFIES.

Just in the wrong direction.

What I was hoping to become playful flirting, somehow takes a turn and becomes an endless back and forth that eventually leads to insults.

I get under her skin and God knows she gets under mine.

I'm hoping that one of these arguments will spark something between us, but upon further investigating, and by that, I mean I observe her shoot down practically every single guy in the office; I learn she has a boyfriend. Some guy from Atlanta she'd been seeing for a hot minute.

Who starts seeing someone right before they move?

That only irritates me more, and that irritation blossoms into what some would call hate, but it isn't. I don't hate Lauren. She pushes my buttons and infuriates me in a way no one has before, but she also pushes me to be a better journalist. She's smart as fuck and has that intuition that can't be taught. It's intrinsic, which is why she's a good fucking reporter. I hate how much I've learned from her in such a short period of time.

I hate how she makes me think.

How she questions every single thing.

How she misses nothing.

But most importantly, I hate how much I want her.

Present Day

"That whole time?" she asks before pressing her forehead to mine. "You fought with me because you had feelings for me? My God, could you be any more cliché?" She smiles, my guess in an attempt to soothe the sting of her words. "So, I *was* the woman you wanted but couldn't have."

"You knew that anyway." I press my lips to her collarbone and she shakes her head.

"You were so mean though…almost cruel. Why didn't you tell me?"

"You had a boyfriend and I didn't want to make things complicated." I shrug.

"So, you fought relentlessly with me instead?"

"Our fighting made us better journalists. We were constantly trying to one up each other and we got better. I was addicted to that. To the high that came from our arguing. You made me better."

"You're insane, you know that?" She chuckles and shakes her head.

"I hadn't meant to be cruel, Lauren. I only wanted to push you, so you'd push me. Yes, there were times you really pissed me off, but for the most part, it was just to get the reaction. And okay the boyfriend thing played a part. I couldn't have you so I figured making you hate me wouldn't hurt."

"You know a lot of people say the opposite of love isn't hate, it's indifference. We had these passionate, explosive responses to each other because…" She bites her lip and looks away from me and I grab her chin.

"Because something's been there from the beginning."

She swallows and nods. "I felt something...I just ignored it."

"Our fighting was the best foreplay I've ever had." She begins to ride my dick again, harder and faster as if this new revelation has ignited something within her.

"I want you," she murmurs. "I've wanted you for a long time, I just haven't wanted to admit it."

"Fuck." I groan. My cock swells, preparing to shoot jets of cum inside of her. "Can I come inside? Tell me now." I don't know that I'll have the power to leave her warm slick pussy so I'm grateful she's controlling this ride.

"Inside." She moans as her lips capture mine and she moves up my shaft one final time before slamming down on top of me. She bites my bottom lip, sucking it into her mouth and I explode inside of her.

"Fuck. Baby, yes." I grit out as her pussy clamps down around me. She milks my cock of every drop, fucking me through my orgasm and even moments after when I feel like I might pass out.

She stops riding me and slides herself off of me but stays straddling my dick, rubbing her slick pussy against me. "You're so fucking perfect," I tell her as I push her wavy hair back out of her face. The water hitting the tile splashes against us and I can tell it's getting cool after being in here close to half an hour.

"So...we are doing this? You and me? How's it going to be with us working together?"

I grab her face, bringing her lips to mine. "Simple. We fight at work and fuck at home."

LAUREN AND I FINALLY MANAGE TO GET DRESSED AND SHE reluctantly prepares to leave to meet up with Charlotte. "I'll try to sneak off when I can," she tells me as she snuggles against my side, fully dressed and all I want is to fuck her for the next few hours.

"Go. Be with your friend. I'll be fine." I press my lips to hers. "I'll be here when you get back."

She whimpers under my lips, and I swallow the sexy sound. I nibble on her bottom lip, desperate to hear it again but she giggles instead. "I should go before I'm naked again." She sits up and moves off the bed, grabbing her purse and downing the rest of the champagne she hadn't finished. She blows a kiss in my direction and then she's gone.

11

LAUREN

I feel like I'm floating down the hallway towards
Charlotte's room. My lips tingle, my sex thumps
with each step and I've got a body high that I feel
from the top of my head to the tips of my toes. I stop in
front of Charlotte's room and let out a breath before
knocking excitedly. I can't wait to tell Charley everything, and despite it being her wedding weekend, I
know she wants to hear every sordid detail of my affair
with Vince.

I knock again, wondering if maybe she left when the
door swings open to Will pulling his shirt over his torso
and his glasses over his eyes.

"Really? Shouldn't you be elsewhere, not seeing the
bride?"

He chuckles before pulling me into a hug. Will and I
have always gotten along really well. We've bonded over

how fiercely protective we are of Charley, and not surprisingly, that bond is strong.

"You know I can't go too long without seeing Charley. How's it going, Lauren?"

I smile thinking about how true his words are. Despite how their affair started with rushed encounters and secret phone calls, Will and Charlotte rarely leave each other's side now. I'd never seen a man and woman love each other so intensely, and they have no shame about sharing their love with the world after having to keep it hidden behind closed doors for so long.

"Really good. Chicago is looking up by the minute," I giggle. I walk by him in time to see Charley brushing her hair into a ponytail. "And where is my goddaughter?"

"With Diana," she tells me. "Mommy and Daddy needed a moment alone." She says as she shares a look with Will I know all too well.

"So, you left her alone with the ice queen?" I ask turning back to Will. It is no secret, at least to me, that he doesn't have the best relationship with his parents, so I'm shocked to learn he'd let his precious baby girl alone with two people that made his childhood miserable.

"Shitty parents make good grandparents, who would have thought?" Will says. "I only give them an hour at a time. Once she's older and she can articulate what's happening over there, I'll consider letting her go for longer." He looks at his phone and then at Charlotte. "I'm going to get her."

She nods and hops up, pressing her lips to his. "I love you." She hugs him like she's not going to see him within an hour and he hugs her back just as tightly.

"I can't wait to marry you," he murmurs against her lips and she squeals with excitement.

"Oh my God. Tomorrow!" She kisses him one final time and grabs my hand. "Now, go. I need to catch up with my girl and learn all about this guy."

Will flashes me a grin. "You're glowing."

"I'm happy."

He nods and I search his face for any sign that maybe he's going to take his brother's side, but I see nothing. "My brother's an idiot."

"I won't hold it against you." I wink.

I'm staring in the mirror at the form fitting black dress that hits just below my knees, and cock my head to the side to stare at the two different shoes on my feet. I raise one leg and then the other, trying to decide which looks better when Vince comes up behind me, running his hand down my side and pressing me against him. "Those." He points at my right foot. "Please tell me I can fuck you in those later."

"You can fuck me in whatever you want, *whenever* you want." I turn around and face him before sliding both heels off. After giving Charlotte all the details about me and Vince, I came back to the room to find him passed out on the bed, so I decided to wake him with my lips wrapped around his cock which then led to another shower and countless orgasms.

"Whenever, huh?" He grabs my ass and squeezes hard.

I shake my head, pushing him off playfully. "Except now. We are going to be late for the rehearsal dinner." I laugh as I grab his hand and look him over. He's wearing a black suit without a tie and a white crisp shirt which I'm sure he'd worn for my benefit after learning how much that simple look turns me on. I bite my lip as a flash of sliding those pants down his legs floats through my mind.

"The way you're looking at me, it doesn't seem you care about being late." He raises my chin to meet his gaze and I smile when I meet his eyes.

How had I missed the way he looks at me this whole time? Was I that oblivious?

Later. I mouth and he nods once before pressing a kiss to my hand.

"You look beautiful by the way."

"You look pretty good yourself, Maddox." I smile before sliding my shoes on. "Alright, it's showtime." I let out a breath, mentally preparing myself for Drew and his whole family.

"Hey," he stops me from moving towards the door, "I got you." He grabs my face and kisses my lips gently. "You're mine now, so the only one allowed to give you a hard time for anything is *me.*"

"OH MY GOD, LAUREN!" DIANA MONTGOMERY, WILL and Drew's mother, is the first to see me the second Vince and I step off the elevator. Chanel Number 5 engulfs me as she steps away from a group of women all dressed in similar attire. As always, Diana is dressed to the nines and channeling Jackie O.

She kisses both of my cheeks and links her arm with mine, pulling me along. I wave a hand towards Vince telling him to follow closely. "I was just beside myself when I heard about you and my son. I truly thought you two were going to make it. A fool he was to let you go." She runs a hand through my hair and tucks a hair behind my ears. She stops walking and looks at Vince as if she's just noticing the six-foot man walking behind us. "And who's this?" She looks at me, and I bite my bottom lip unsure of exactly what to call him.

"Vince Maddox, ma'am," Vince answers for me. "I'm a friend of Lauren's from work." He shakes her hand, pressing his lips to the top, and surprisingly I spot a faint blush painting her cheeks. Though she composes herself quickly.

"A friend, huh?" She raises an eyebrow at me and I try not to look guilty when I shouldn't. Drew dumped *me*. More importantly, Drew dumped *me* for another woman. "You give him hell." She taps my nose. "This new girl he's with is just…" she sighs and rubs her forehead, "unpolished to say the least." I giggle because I know Diana Montgomery pretty well, and a woman that doesn't understand how to move in social settings is basically a leper in her eyes.

"I mean really, who could follow me?" I joke.

She smiles and gives me a hug. "No one. You're one of a kind."

"So is Charlotte, you know. You really haven't laid off her yet?" It's a plain truth that Diana favors me over her future daughter-in-law which is how I get away with talking so candidly. "She even gave you a grand-daughter. You're going to have to forgive her for being married when she met your son." I shoot her a pointed look and she throws her hands up in exasperation.

"She cost him his career!"

"There were two people involved if I recall, and Will is doing great. He's happy. They're happy. You keep pushing them and they're going to limit your time with Ana and the rest of the basketball team you know they're going to have."

She frowns. "She's growing on me."

"Grow faster."

She smiles at me and shakes her head before turning to Vince. "Look after this one, alright?" She doesn't wait for his response before she floats into the room where we're having the rehearsal dinner.

"Your ex's mom?"

"Mmmhmmm."

"She likes you." I try to gauge his reaction to this piece of information but he gives nothing away.

"I'm likable."

"So, you think." He shoots me a sideways look and I slap his shoulder playfully. I let out a deep breath as we make our way into the room where people are casually mingling. There is a cocktail hour happening before dinner, serving as a meet and greet, and I know Will and Charley are both nervous about their extended families mixing for the first time.

I spot Charley in a white backless dress that makes her skin practically glow, and of course, Will right next to her, his hand rubbing her back slowly as he holds their daughter in the other.

I spot J.R., Will and Drew's father next, as he's one of those men that knows how to command a room. He's in the center of the massive space with five other men, all wearing power suits and sipping whiskey, waiting for the moment that they can make their exit to smoke their Cuban cigars and talk some patriarchal bullshit, I'm sure.

I don't necessarily dislike their father, I've just always felt that he's...well, an asshole. It seems he liked Charley a touch more than Diana, but it hadn't stopped him from bringing up the idea of her signing a prenuptial agreement.

Will had a fit over that.

"You want a drink?" Vince whispers in my ear and it's amazing how easily his voice calms my nerves. I turn towards him and cock my hips to one side, putting a hand on one hip.

"A friend from work?"

"Did you want to announce to the entire wedding party that I'm eating your pussy on the regular? I'm confused, she seemed pretty concerned with tact."

I scowl at his sarcasm, not particularly in the mood for it while I'm this tense and more importantly, this sober. "You could have said boyfriend."

"Am I your boyfriend? I didn't even know *you* were calling me that."

"Are we really defining the relationship *now?*" I ask as we move towards the bar nestled in the corner of the room. He orders us two Manhattans and I'm grateful for the strength of the drink as it cools my dry mouth.

I haven't spotted Drew yet, but I know it's only a matter of time before we have that awkward encounter, and I can only hope that I'll be somewhat intoxicated.

I move towards the head table where I know we are seated from helping Charley set up earlier and set my clutch down at my seat. "And guest, huh?" He picks up the gold place card and I giggle as I run my hand over the white tablecloth.

"The place cards were finished when we decided you'd be joining me."

I take a sip of my drink and make the mistake of looking up at the exact moment Drew enters the room to find his eyes on me. I stiffen under his harsh gaze and I feel Vince's hand wrap around my waist. "Relax, baby."

"He's pissed at me."

"You expected that." I've looked away but I can feel his eyes on me and Vince. "You okay?"

"It's weird, right? I'm sorry I brought you into this." There is a storm brewing and I can only hope that Vince and I don't get caught in the wreckage.

"Hey, I brought myself into it, remember? It's fine." He runs his hand down my bare shoulder and pulls me into his arms before pressing a kiss behind my ear. "I've got you, remember?" I shiver in his arms and emboldened by the whiskey and maybe because I also want to show my ex I've moved on, I press my lips to his.

"Thank you." I smile up at him when a deep voice interrupts us.

"Lauren Michaels." I look to the right and spot Drew's father staring at me over his drink, with an unlit cigar planted between his index and middle finger.

"Hi, J.R." I make my way around the table to let him pull me into a hug. "How are you?"

"Can't complain. How's the Windy City?"

"Amazing. Best choice I could have made." I watch him size up Vince before turning back to me. I'm wondering if he's going to ask about the man who's making his way to stand behind me when that storm shifts dramatically in my direction.

"J.R." Drew Montgomery, who's easily Vince's height, with blonde hair and light eyes, slaps his father's back and stares at me. "Lauren."

"Hi, Drew." I feel Vince behind me instantly, and I wonder if he's feeling out the situation because he doesn't touch me. I'm not sure if I'm relieved or disappointed.

He takes a sip of his drink as his eyes flit from me to the man behind me. I can see he wants to say something, but he just shakes his head and turns to his dad. "Mom wants to talk to you."

He nods at both of us before they make a swift, quiet exit that's full of meaning. I let out a breath I hadn't realized I'd been holding before I feel his hand at my back. "He wants you back."

"What?" I spin around and look up at Vince. His blue eyes are intense but I see the vulnerability behind them as well. "I don't want him back."

"I didn't say you did. I just know what it's like to get dumped and have them come crawling back. It's a heady, powerful feeling and it's easy to get sucked back in even if it's not what you want."

I let his words soak in. He's right; the idea of Drew wanting me back after he'd broken my heart and humiliated me by flaunting his new girlfriend all over Atlanta in front of our mutual friends does make me feel a bit lighter. But I don't want him.

"I want you," I tell him honestly. "Not him."

His arm wraps around me as he drags his nose down my cheek. "You smell so fucking good."

I giggle and we move back around the table to take our seats as I notice Will and Charley make their way to the center of the room with a microphone. Traditionally, the groom's father makes a toast at the rehearsal dinner, but I'm sure Will and Charley shut the idea down of J.R. speaking publicly without a second thought.

Charley winks at me and gives me a tiny wave as she rocks Ana in her arms and lifts her tiny arm to wave at me. I wave back and I feel Vince's hand trail up my thigh. "You want kids?"

I look to my left, which unfortunately is towards Drew who's sitting at the opposite end of the table and I can sense his scowl directed at us. "Yes, one day."

"All girls if Scarlett is correct?"

"I can't believe Scarlett put that into the universe. I *cannot* have all girls. I'll die. We're a handful." The idea of having all girls, with my sass and stubbornness has my anxiety rising by the second and simultaneously blessing the man that ends up being their father.

"If they're all like you, I'd have to agree with that." He chuckles. "They'd be gorgeous though."

I'm about to respond when Will's voice quiets the room. "On behalf of my future bride, our daughter, and myself, I'd like to thank each of you for joining us tonight and tomorrow as we celebrate our marriage. It hasn't been the easiest journey to get here, but I'd like to think we are stronger for it. I'd like to thank Charlotte's family for embracing me and her mother, Carla for taking me in like a son."

"Yeah, her second one." Drew snorts and I snap my eyes angrily to his brother. I don't think many people heard it outside of our table, but I spy Charlotte flinch, so I'm fairly certain she did. I know Drew loves Charlotte, and there haven't been any issues between them so I'm confused as to why he felt the need to make that comment. But my guess is he's pissed at her for taking away his plus one and giving one to me.

"Wow." Vince murmurs under his breath and I shake my head.

"Fucking asshole."

Will, who didn't seem to miss a beat, finishes his speech, gives a toast, kisses Charley and his daughter, and just when everyone turns to their meals he casually strolls to our table towards his brother and grips his shoulder. He lowers his face between him and another groomsman, and though I see the smile on his lips, I see the anger in his eyes, and then they're on the move towards the door.

"Dick," Charlotte grumbles as she sits down in the chair next to me with Ana perched in her lap. "Do you think everyone heard?"

"No no," I shake my head, "just us and maybe the table over."

I can see her eyes glisten slightly but she blinks them away. "That was so humiliating."

"Hey, stop. That's not about you." I wrap an arm around her and kiss her temple.

"Will is pissed." Charley bites her bottom lip as Ana grips her finger. She pulls her close to her chest and kisses her forehead and it makes my heart swell with how much she loves her daughter. Charley was always destined to be a mother and she's assumed the role so beautifully. There is nothing she loves more than her little family and it shows.

"Of course, Hot Doc will go to battle for you one hundred times over against anyone. You know that."

"I just never expected it would be with Drew." Her face falls slightly. "It's the night before our wedding and he's the best man."

"Hey, everything is going to be fine. That is not your concern. Your concern is getting down that aisle tomorrow and marrying the love of your life and then working on baby number two."

Her eyes widen in horror as she shakes her head. "Oh God no, we're waiting another year. Ana is barely one!"

Will comes back to the table and sits next to Charlotte, grabbing her hand instantly. "Da!" Ana reaches for him and Charley lets her climb into his lap.

"Everything okay?" Charley asks and Will nods before pressing a kiss to her lips.

"Nothing for you to worry about, baby. He's just drunk." He rubs Ana's back and begins kissing her tiny face causing her to burst into the happiest giggles.

Charlotte smiles, distracted momentarily by their adorable daughter before turning back to him. "Where is he now?"

"I told him he needed to cool off before he came back in."

It doesn't appear he got that memo, though, because

moments later he appears and sits down at the table with another glass full to the brim of what I assume to be whiskey. Our eyes meet, his full of anger and mine full of disappointment.

AN HOUR, A FEW MORE DRINKS, AND QUITE POSSIBLY THE best meal I've ever had later, I head to the lady's room. I never even thought that Drew would use this time to approach me when I'm without Vince or Charlotte, but I should have expected it.

"You really brought that asshole here? I thought you hated him, or was that all just to hide the fact that you were messing around with him? Were you fucking him when we were together?" I hear just as I emerge from the lady's room. I look to the right to see Drew sitting on a couch, nursing yet another drink before he gets up and makes his way towards me. His body is tense and rigid, and I know it's only a matter of time before he blows up as he tends to do when he drinks too much.

"You should really stop drinking and switch to water or go lie down in your room before you embarrass yourself even further."

"You know what the fuck is embarrassing? Is you showing up to *my* brother's wedding with a date a month after we broke up after you bitched to Charlotte about me bringing a date? How fucking bitter are you? And you've yet to answer my question."

"Well, first of all, it's insulting. I never cheated on you, so no, Vince and I started after you dumped me. Speaking of which, were you fucking the girl you left me for when *we* were together?" I hate that I want to know, and I hate myself even more for asking when he's clearly going to lie through his teeth.

"No. Well…" he runs his tongue over his teeth, "she slept over once, but nothing happened."

I feel like someone's punched me in the gut. *What the fuck does that even mean? Let's just say for argument's sake, I did believe that, so what he's telling me is they spent the whole night fucking cuddling?* I swallow down the bile in my throat and take a step back. "Don't ever speak to me again."

I attempt to walk by him but he grabs my arm, not hard but enough to stop me in my tracks and I look down at where he's holding me. "Is that prick in there just to make me jealous?"

"If he is, clearly it worked," I snap. "You're so jealous, you can't even see straight."

"Of course, I am." He grits out. "You're here… looking like *that* with some asshole that doesn't even like you or respect you."

I'm about to respond when broad shoulders block my view. "That's enough." Vince's voice is cold, almost sinister, and despite spending the better part of six months locked in war, I've never heard him speak like that.

"Who the fuck asked you? I'm talking to Lauren." He

tries to step around him to get a better look at me but Vince just moves with him, keeping me out of his view.

"And now you're talking to *me*. I don't know how you and Will are brothers because it's like fucking night and day. Let me tell you something, *bro*. Lauren has moved on. She doesn't want you, and she certainly doesn't want to hear some pathetic sob story about how you fucked up. And you are certainly one to talk to *anyone* about respect. You broke up with her via text so you could fuck some ho? And you thought you two could just hook up this weekend as some sort of parting gift? Grow up."

"I don't owe you any fucking explanation," Drew spits out. "Lauren knows how I feel about her."

"Well, lucky for me, she no longer gives a fuck."

"Screw you. Lauren used to talk a lot of fucking shit about you. She hated you and what? Now you're together? Please."

"What goes on between Lauren and I is none of your fucking business. Now, I'm advising you to walk away." He takes a step closer. "I only give one warning." Goosebumps appear all over my arms at this side of Vince I've never seen. Venom drips from his voice and I gasp quietly hearing how protective and possessive he is. "You had your chance and you fucked up. So now, Lauren is *mine*."

VINCE

I am livid as fuck as I stare down my woman's drunk ex-boyfriend who seems to think he can drive a wedge between us. He takes a step towards me, not heeding my warnings, so that we're almost toe to toe. He's about my height so we're eye to eye, and the look in his is one of anger but also of what I believe to be sadness. He knows he fucked up by breaking up with Lauren and he's pissed that she hasn't been sitting in Chicago crying over him for the past month. That she's moved on *with me*.

I'm half expecting him to take a swing at me when Will's voice thunders down the hallway. "What's going on?"

Drew takes a step back and crosses his arms. "Just having a little chat with Lauren's fucktoy." He chuckles. "Everything's good, baby bro."

"Stop it." I hear from behind me. "Drew, you're

drunk and you need to go to bed." Lauren moves from behind me and immediately I put an arm in front of her, shielding her from this man whose behavior I can't predict. I don't think he'd get aggressive with Lauren, but I can't take any chances.

"Lauren's right, Drew. You're making an ass of yourself, and I get it, you're pissed off, but you just need to sleep it off. You'll feel better in the morning." Will seems to be level headed and I'm wondering if it's because I haven't seen him consume one alcoholic beverage. I don't think I've seen Charley drink anything either. *Do they not drink? Maybe just because of Ana.*

"I fucked up, Lauren," Drew finally says and Will pulls him back slightly.

"Not the time, Drew."

"No, it is. Lauren, I'm sorry. I was a dick." He shakes his head and, in this moment, I almost feel bad for him. It's obvious he's still in love with her. "The distance just sucked. I missed you so much and you were always busy. Always working. I felt like you didn't even care about our relationship."

"I cared." Her voice is small and timid and I wonder if it's because she doesn't want to have this conversation with him in front of me. "I loved you."

"Loved?" he asks, his eyes meet hers and all of the anger and hate from earlier seems to have disappeared. "Past tense?"

"Yes. Drew…we started growing apart the second I moved here. You could feel it and so could I. Maybe things would have been different if you moved with me, but I think this was inevitable."

"I can move to Chicago; we can start over," he pleads, and my eyes dart to Lauren, wanting to observe her body language as she answers this question. I knew what she'd say, but did she mean it?

She shakes her head and surprisingly slides her hand through mine, lacing our fingers. "No, we can't Drew... I've moved on."

He looks at me and then down at our conjoined hands. "So quickly?"

"You moved on quicker than I did," she counters.

"She doesn't mean anything to me." Drew shakes his head and I almost chuckle at his fuckboy attitude. *He really does have a lot of growing up to do.*

"That's not the point," Lauren says. "Even if there isn't another woman," she pauses and looks up at me, "there's another man." There's no smile on her lips, but I can see it in her eyes, feel it in the way she squeezes my hand and leans closer to me.

He takes a step back and looks at his brother who gives him a look of support. "Let's go take a walk, get you some water." He wraps an arm around his shoulder and pulls him back further.

Drew finally admits defeat, letting his head hang low and nods slowly as the two of them walk down the hall-way. Once they're out of sight, Lauren is in my arms, pulling my face to hers and kissing me hard and desper-ately. "I am so sorry."

137

"Don't be, I told you I got you." I hold her tight in my arms and brush my nose against hers gently.

She pulls back slightly and winces. "I know, but that was ridiculous. When he drinks too much, he becomes a wildcard and gets super aggressive. It's never been towards me but he just...gets like that."

"I anticipated some sort of pissing match. To be honest, I thought he was going to hit me and then I'd feel really guilty for hitting him back and giving him a black eye for all of the wedding pictures."

Lauren's eyes widen and she puts a hand over her mouth to suppress a giggle. "Oh my God, I didn't even think of that. Charley and Will would understand though. Will still beats himself up that he didn't get to hit Charley's first husband at least *once*."

"Oh shit. He knew Charley's first husband?" I don't know the story about what happened, but Lauren has mentioned a few times that her first husband wasn't the best of men.

"Oh my God. Wait till you hear that story."

THE SOUND OF KNOCKING WAKES ME UP FROM SLEEP, AND I'm surprised to find Lauren's warm naked curves are no longer pressed against me like they were for the majority of the night. I'd woken up a few times throughout the night because Lauren shifts in her sleep and rubs against my cock nonstop. *Even when she's*

unconscious, she torments me. I sit up slightly when I hear voices at the door but I can't see who it is. I pull on my sweats and a t-shirt and move closer to the door to hear Drew's voice loud and clear. I'm not ready to make my presence known quite yet, but I do want to hear what he has to say now that he's more sober and sentient.

"I'm sorry for being such an asshole last night, Lauren. It was just…difficult seeing you with someone else." His voice sounds hoarse and he clears his throat.

"I get that."

"I don't want to ruin Charlotte and Will's day, so you don't have to worry about a repeat of last night."

"Well, I would hope not. You're the best man and his older brother and I'm the maid of honor; I would hope we could put our differences aside to celebrate two people that mean a lot to us."

"We can, Lauren, I'm sorry."

"Okay, I apologize as well if you felt ambushed by me bringing Vince. It wasn't my intention, I just…" I raise an eyebrow because it was kind of her intention, though us confessing our feelings for each other, thereby making *me* possessive as hell, probably wasn't. "Vince came out of nowhere. I wasn't expecting any of this to happen, you know."

There's a bit of silence and just when I'm about to make myself visible to both of them Lauren speaks up. "I have to start getting ready."

"Right, me too. Will scheduled us an eleven am tee

time." He groans. "I'm hungover as hell and he wants to go play golf."

Lauren chuckles. "Have fun!"

The door closes and Lauren comes into view and gives me a knowing smile. "How long did you know I was standing here," I ask her as I pull her into my arms.

"Long enough." She smiles and wraps her arms around my neck.

"He full of shit?" I ask about Drew's apology.

"No, I don't think so. Besides, Diana probably gave him hell last night for getting belligerent. I'm sure she'll keep him in check today. Do you care either way?"

"Not particularly, I just don't want him bothering you anymore."

"Hmmm, I'm thinking I'll be a distant memory once I'm back in Chicago."

"I doubt it. I haven't stopped thinking about you since the moment I saw you in the elevator." I run my hands down her body and cup her ass.

She narrows her eyes at me. "Or when you spent a full week calling me Laura?"

"Okay, you know I was just fucking around with you."

She looks behind me towards the bed and then back at me before shooting me a cheeky grin. "I don't have to be in Charley's room for another hour, do you want to fuck around with me now?"

EPILOGUE

LAUREN

Three Years Later

"A untie Lo, Auntie Lo!!!" Emma comes running through the suite waving a small piece of paper in her hand. I cringe thinking about her getting her dress dirty and luckily, my sister sees the apprehension all over my face and grabs her hand.

"What did we tell you about running in your dress? You don't want to get it dirty before everyone sees how pretty you look in it, right?" She kneels down in front of her to brush her fluffy white dress and fixes the flowers in her hair.

"But Mommy, look! Uncle V sent her a note!" I turn my head to the side hearing her mention *Uncle V,* also known as my soon to be husband, Vincent. My mother had just set my veil in place and they had sprayed my face with setting spray so my makeup wouldn't move and now Vince is about to shoot that all to hell with his *last note to the bride*.

Emma places it in my lap and gives me a smile. "He said make sure no one gets this but you."

"Did he pay you for your transportation services?" I ask her.

She holds up a five dollar bill with a smile. "You know it!"

I chuckle at the bond Emma and Vince have and it makes my heart flutter over how much they adore each other making me excited for when we have our own babies. The room clears out to give me a second alone with the exception of my mother, Charley, and the photographer as I open the note that Vince sent.

The Future Mrs. Maddox,

Who would have thought we'd finally get here, huh? I honestly thought I was going to have to force you down the aisle with how long you made me wait for today. You have been the love of my life for so long and I can't wait to make you officially mine. I can't wait to see your beautiful face and kiss those perfect lips. So, let's get this show on the road, I'm ready when you are.

(Though, let's be honest, I was ready two and a half years ago.)

I love you forever, Michaels.
VM

I smile through the tears as I read his note a few times wondering how in the world I got to be this happy. I look up at my mom and give her a smile before letting my eyes float upwards, wishing my father were here to walk me down the aisle before letting her pull me to my feet.

"He would have loved Vince." She tells me as she dabs a tissue underneath my eye, to wipe the tears building. "He's so proud of you, Lauren."

"I hope so." I nod as she clasps my hand and we make our way out of the bridal suite toward the garden where I'll be marrying Vincent Maddox, ex-co-worker, enemy turned lover turned love of my life. We decided to get married in Atlanta, not wanting to rely on temperamental Chicago weather to behave for what we both wanted to be an outdoor wedding. The weather is gorgeous, a perfect day in May that isn't too hot or too cold and not a cloud in sight. My sister has just made her way down the aisle when my mother grabs my hand and gives it a squeeze. "You ready?"

"Been ready."

I'm prepared to lock eyes with Vince the second he turns around when something else catches my eye. In the back row, in a seat furthest from the aisle, I spot a familiar face.

Scarlett Stone.

I pause, not wanting to misstep when I meet her gaze, wondering if she's a wedding crasher or if Vince invited her without me knowing as a fun surprise. I smile and shake my head, the tears welling in my eyes that she predicted our romance years ago, claiming that it was "written in the stars," which neither of us believed at the time. She nods her head at me and just before I turn my head to proceed down the aisle, she winks.

Five Years Later

"Claire Victoria Maddox!" I call out for my very rambunctious four-year-old who refuses to sit still as she runs around the hotel suite.

"Mommy!" She runs towards me, preparing to jump into my lap before Vince grabs her and pulls her into his arms.

"Mommy is wearing a very pretty white dress, and we talked about being careful and not jumping on Mommy, right?" I stand up revealing the small bump in my stomach that housed our second child. *Another daughter.*

"Yes, no jumping. I wasn't going to, Daddy, I promise!" Claire, who's the spitting image of her father with slightly darker blonde hair and light-colored eyes that sometimes look blue and sometimes look green, squeezes his cheeks together and plants a kiss on his lips. "Can I have cake now?"

"As soon as Mommy and Daddy get married again." I

smile at his words and my heart flutters at his romantic idea to renew our vows on our five-year anniversary.

"Yay!" She kicks her legs against him before she jumps down and runs out of the room screaming for Vince's mother.

"How is my bride doing?" he asks as he makes his way towards me.

"Good, a little sick." I scrunch my nose after spending this morning with my head in the toilet. I'd had little to no morning sickness with Claire, but this second one… *My God.* I'm ready for this trimester to be over.

He drops to one knee in front of me and presses his lips to my stomach. "Baby…Mommy and Daddy have very important plans today, and for the next few days." He looks up at me with a wicked grin. "Can you maybe give Mommy a little break?"

I giggle when he presses his lips to the area and stands back up and cups my cheeks gently. "I love you so much."

"I love you, too." I rub my nose against his, like we always do and he presses his lips to my nose.

"Let's go get married again."

We're just about to move towards the garden in Atlanta where we'd gotten married the first time when Claire comes running back in. "Mommy Mommy! You have something." She hands me a small envelope with just my name written on the front in script.

"From you?" I ask wondering if my husband is

redoing everything he did five years ago, including the note he sent me moments before I walked down the aisle.

"No, actually."

I open the envelope and read the few words written in pink before we both burst out laughing.

I told you.
Two marriages!
Xo, Scarlett Stone

THE END

ALSO BY Q.B. TYLER

My Best Friend's Sister

Unconditional

Forget Me Not

BITTERSWEET DUET

Bittersweet Surrender

Bittersweet Addiction

CAMPUS TALES SERIES

First Semester

Second Semester

Spring Semester

ABOUT THE AUTHOR

Hailing from the Nation's Capital, Q.B. Tyler, spends her days constructing her "happily ever afters" with a twist, featuring sassy heroines and the heroes that worship them. But most importantly the love story that develops despite *inconvenient* circumstances.

Sign up for her <u>newsletter</u> to stay in touch

BB bookbub.com/profile/q-b-tyler

facebook.com/author.qbtyler

instagram.com/author.qbtyler

twitter.com/qbtyler

ACKNOWLEDGMENTS

This book wouldn't… *couldn't* have happened without some pretty fabulous people. Your input, your love, your support is invaluable to me. As I, (and Carrie Bradshaw) have said probably a million times—sometimes family is the one you're born into, and sometimes it's the one you make for yourself.

Carmel Rhodes, Erica Marselas and Melissa Spence Thank you for reading every word and all of your feedback even when I send chapters in the middle of the night! Thank you for loving Lauren and Vince as much as I do!

Kristen Portillo, with every book I swear it gets better, and it's because of you both! Your magic never ceases to amaze me!

Harlow Layne, Helen Hadjia, Kelsey Cheyenne, Danielle James, Gemini Jensen, Rose Croft, Jeanette

Piastri and Alexis Rae, Thank you for being a sounding board, a safe space and my tribe. I love being on this journey with you guys! So much love.

Denise Reyes, I am so freaking grateful for you. You've taken on so many roles at this point, I don't even know where to start thanking you. For beta reading this. For keeping me going. For talking with me about everything book related and for being in a different time zone which means I can message you at two in the morning and you'll see it! For running my street team. Gah! My love for you is endless! Thank you so much!

My Street Team Babes: What was I doing before you all came along? You guys have changed my writing career for the better and I love you so much! Your enthusiasm, your excitement, your support means everything to me. I don't think I can say that enough. A million thank yous!

Author loves: I'm so lucky to know so many of you and I can't thank you enough for your friendship and advice and support! I can't wait to meet so many more of you in just a few weeks!

To everyone in the Hive, I love you! Some of you have been with me, what, almost five years? Where does the time go? Thank you for your love and your support and making me feel like I *can*.

And finally, to the readers: Thank you for going on yet another journey with me. You guys rock my world every day!

Printed in Great Britain
by Amazon

82612056R00092